Fred. W. Waithman

Indolent Impressions

Sketches in Light and Shade

Fred. W. Waithman

Indolent Impressions
Sketches in Light and Shade

ISBN/EAN: 9783337013851

Printed in Europe, USA, Canada, Australia, Japan

Cover: Foto ©Andreas Hilbeck / pixelio.de

More available books at **www.hansebooks.com**

INDOLENT IMPRESSIONS

Sketches in Light and Shade

BY

FRED. W. WAITHMAN

LONDON

DIGBY, LONG & CO., Publishers

18 BOUVERIE STREET, FLEET STREET, E.C.

1895

CONTENTS

—:o:—

THE DISADVANTAGES OF RESPECTABILITY.

THERE are few people in this world, outside the criminal classes, but have at some period of their lives felt a desire to enter that portion of society at large labelled "respectable." But many having got there after a hard struggle, have not unfrequently wished themselves well out of the thraldom imposed upon the not too wealthy members of the respectable portion of the great middle-class community of the British Isles.

Respectability on a limited income is indeed a hard and trying thing to keep up, and many a man has found himself compelled to submit to the degradation of a private arrangement with his creditors from no other cause than the difficulty of maintaining a respectable appearance on an

A

income totally inadequate to the require-
ments of a middle-class respectability.

Take the case of a young married man
holding a position as clerk in a mercantile
establishment of standing and repute.   He
is expected to be respectable in appearance,
to turn up in the regulation costume of respectability, and to reside in a respectable
quarter of the town or district in which he
is employed.   All this is necessary to give him
any chance of advancement in his business;
for if he once show signs of seediness or
necessity, he is sure to be sneered at by his
fellow-clerks, and passed over by his superiors.

Therefore, the semblance of respectability
means to him the keeping of his position
and the possibility of advancement.   Away
from his employment he is still haunted by
the bugbear of respectability.   His wife—
and children, if he have any—must be
respectably dressed at all seasons and times,
and his house must present a respectable
appearance outside and in.

The very appearance in question will, as likely as not, determine the attention or inattention he will receive at the hands of his medical attendant, and will also help to reassure any creditor who, having to wait for his money owing to illness, may call to inquire about his "small account." And all this has generally to be done on a salary totally inadequate to the demands of respectability. What is the result?

The discovery that respectability has the most distinct and unpleasant disadvantages if it be not fully backed up by an adequate supply of that necessary evil—money. Respectability on a limited income means constant anxiety and constant self-denial. It means worry and inconvenience, and if many a worn-out wife and wearied husband were truthfully to state the cause of their troubles, they would unhesitatingly answer —"respectability."

Respectability too frequently means pinching to make ends meet, contriving and ar-

ranging to convince the world that you
are not hard-up, and a constant state of
false appearances before the light of respectability's criticisms, which is, alas, too
often paid for when the light is off by a
hand-to-mouth existence of a far from
pleasant nature.

Not only is the small salaried clerk
made to feel keenly the disadvantages of
respectability, but others in better social
positions know as well as he does what a
thorny path the high road of respectability
may be. Take the vicar with a moderate
stipend, a family, and constant calls on his
purse from the varied channels of a poor
and crowded parish. He is expected to
maintain a good social position, to keep
his wife and children well-dressed, and to
give the latter an education befitting their
social standing and respectability. He is
frequently compelled to pay a curate, and
has to help his parish poor, and visit
with and receive the best society in the

district of which he has spiritual charge. No one knows better than this man what are the disadvantages of respectability, for he not only has them painfully and practically demonstrated by his own daily life, but he comes into constant contact with them in his daily round of parish duties.

Much more does his curate, with a smaller stipend than the vicar, feel the calls and responsibilities of respectability, which cripple his desire to help his poorer fellows, and compel him, too often, to think seriously of how he is to make ends meet, without losing caste in the social circle in which he is compelled to move.

Children brought up respectably, and having all done for them that is considered requisite in the matter of education, have no idea of the hours of anxious thought their very respectability has cost their parents, but many a fond father and loving mother could testify to the straits they have at times been put to, for the purpose of enabling them to bring their children up in due accordance with the unwritten but undeviating laws of respectability.

The atmosphere of respectability brings in its train tastes and habits which add considerably to the difficulties of such people as are compelled to keep up the semblance of it under the greatest disadvantages, and there can be no doubt that the workingman is, from many points of view, in a happier condition than is the representative of typical respectability.

For the "clodhopper" appearances have no terrors. He eats, drinks, works and sleeps, and provided he can get enough of this world's goods to keep him out of the workhouse, he is fairly well satisfied. He has no fear of the opinion of respectability, and if he be not possessed of any of the advantages of that state of life, he is at least not troubled with its disadvantages, and he goes on the even tenor of his way with a light pocket and a light heart.

THE morning kiss is not merely the meeting of two mouths. It is the sign manual of a lasting love. To its absence has, ere this, been traced the beginning of a jealousy which ended in two wrecked lives. The kiss—apart from the commodity supplied in schools and families — has long been looked upon as the seal which ratifies the vows of love; and, as everybody knows, it is the usual thing, on the occasion of a maiden giving her heart and hand to a successful wooer, for them to embrace and clinch their amatory bargain with a kiss. From this period the kiss becomes a recognised institution, and the lovers would no more dream of meeting or parting without kissing than they would dream of discussing

the proceedings of the divorce court prior
to the consummation of their marriage.

But it is after that ceremony has been
completed, and they have set out upon their
double-harnessed journey, that the importance of the morning kiss begins to assert
itself.

The newly-made bride looks for her morning kiss with the same regularity that she
looks for the weekly supply of filthy lucre
wherewith she keeps the wheels of the
domestic machinery in working order. And
for a time she has no cause to complain as
to the receipt of it.

But in course of time the husband, with
no direct intention of offence, does not supply
it as regularly as of yore, and it is relegated
to the same oblivion as are many other
small attentions that were wont to sweeten
the halcyon days of courtship.

It is the old tale of familiarity, and without knowing it, he is slowly but surely
sowing the seeds of mistrust and misery.

Women are quick to notice the small things of life, and when they come so near home as to touch their own pride, they soon make mountains out of what other people would consider but mole-hills.

When the husband, with his head full of business cares, evinces a desire to leave home as early as possible in the morning —without the usual kiss—or, on coming home at night tired out, puts on his slippers and, seeking solace in his pipe, sits silently thinking out some commercial problem, his wife imagines she is being neglected, and without going straight to the point and stating her grievance, falls back upon that form of feminine consolation known as sulking.

She does not answer her husband's questions in the old way, and when asked if she is not well, replies with a negative that carries with it all the appearances of an affirmative. Her husband not unnaturally concludes that she is out of temper about something, and failing to elicit any tangible cause for the effect, as likely as not goes off to his club to get out of the way of a brewing storm, and to ruminate over the inconsistencies of womankind and the difference between married life and love-making. The wife meanwhile nurses her secret sorrow, and they gradually drift into a pair of common-place disciples of Hymen, who, while not breaking out into open rebellion, feel that they are not so well suited to each other as they once imagined they were.

And all for the mere omission of the morning kiss.

The process of drifting is an easy but dangerous one, and once commenced is difficult to conquer, and it is usually from causes as slight as these that it is indulged in by men and women who, finding themselves apathetic to what they once adored, seek in fresh fields and pastures new to find a pleasant antidote for their domestic banes.

All men and women are not endowed with the same natures, and the absence of the morning kiss and similar attentions often produces in a woman's heart a yearning for the love she imagines she has not possessed. It is to women of this class that neglect in the matter of affection is so dangerous. They must be loved—or imagine that they are—and the first sign of a slumbering passion is the keynote for the uprising of their souls. Love and adoration they must and will have, and if they find it not within the precincts of their own castles, they promptly, and with no thought of consequences, seek for it elsewhere. They would tell you, and believe it to be true, that they drifted into their fatal error; but those of the world who know their kind, know also that, given what they desire, they do not count its cost or the penalty their action carries with it. They yearn to let their stifled passions have full play, and if at the end of a brief Elysium they find the shadow of unfaithfulness, they still hug to their hearts the thought they have at least been loved and have lived, if only to fall from the heights of Olympus to the depths of Hades.

Nor are women the only sinners in this direction, for men are equally sensitive, and many a man, who thought himself neglected by his wife, has found in another's charms some consolation for his wounded vanity.

Divorce court records but tell the bare facts so far as they concern the law; they seldom, if ever, trace the history of the family skeleton to its true source. As the spring runs on until it merges into the river, so do the trivialities of life provide the mainspring which sets up the rift within the lute, and that frequently from no greater cause than the missing of the morning kiss.

The moral is obvious.

Men more than women should remember

that courtesy costs nothing, and that if the thoughtfulness and attention of their engagement days were but carried into their wedded life, they would have little to fear from the demons of jealousy or apathy. If this were carried out to the full, there would be more happy homes than there are, and thousands of women would worship their husbands who now drag out a hopeless existence instead of trying honestly to do their duty in the sphere of life to which it has pleased God to call them.

HAVING A DRINK.

THE convivial operation known as "having a drink" is one of the most popular customs of this, our Island of England, and if it were only carried out in a reasonable and rational manner it would be one of the pleasantest. But it is not; as many a man can testify to his sorrow, especially when he wakes up "next morning" with a parched throat and a head three sizes too large for his hat.

It is when this feeling comes over him that the average man begins to moralise, and it is strange how confoundedly moral he generally is "next morning." When he comes to reflect how many drinks he consumed during the progress of the day before, he usually arrives at the conclusion that the game is not worth the candle, and that from thence he will, to use a vulgarism, "chuck it up" and reform. And he means it, but the flesh is weak and the spirits of the night before were strong, and as strength invariably overcomes weakness, he decides to "treat resolution" with "just one" to pull himself together prior to commencing his walk along the trying path of temperance or teetotalism. But the primrose path of dalliance is a tempting thoroughfare, and has ere this lured men on when they knew in their heart of hearts that they ought to stick to the road of resolution. He has one drink and tackles it with a firmness of resolution and an unfirmness of hand that look on the face of it a fair sign that he means to depart from the ways of the night before and give it a miss for the future.

But at this particular moment a friend turns up and he feels bound, as a matter of common courtesy, to ask him to "have one," which he promptly does, accompanying the action by an endorsement of his friend's ideas as to the folly of extensive imbibing of alcoholic refreshment. Well, so far, so good, but the second friend feels that he cannot accept a drink without asking his chum to have another in return, so, with emphatic remarks as to this being the last one, they imbibe once more. They are in no particular hurry, and do not feel particularly inclined to face the cares and anxieties of business so early in the morning, and so they sit and chat about things in general, and—as often as not—the chances of certain gee-gees in particular. While this is going on certain other birds-of-a-feather have appeared upon the scene and a commiseration committee is promptly formed by the suffering ones. This is the beginning of the end, and the two resolute reformers are gradually lured back to the old paths they trod the day before. Resolution is routed by companionship, and conversational conviviality reigns supreme.

That any sensible man goes out in the morning with the deliberate intention of getting inebriated is, on the face of it, absurd, but that men do regularly get into that condition without intention is a patent fact. With these it is, as I have pointed out already, companionship and sociability that brings about the undesired result, and so long as men have brains and education so long will they seek to vary the monotony of business life by the relief afforded by the enticing accompaniments of a refresher.

It is, perhaps, no exaggeration to say that a large percentage of ordinary business is done over a morning bitter and its subsequent results, and this is a point that must be a source of annoyance to the rabid teetotaller, who will find it an absolute impossibility to put down drinking so long as commerce and alcohol are combined.

There is no one more intemperate than your platform teetotaller, with his sweeping assertions and his smug hypocrisy,

B

which do more harm to the cause he wishes to urge than he can possibly imagine. That drinking is frequently the cause of misery and poverty I admit, but it will never be put down by the rabid railings of paid advocates. It has become a custom, and if it is an evil it has to some extent become a necessary one. The ordinary drinker does little harm to anyone but himself, and is entirely without the pale of the agitator's condemnation.

The shady side of the drink question is a deeper study, and cannot be treated in the same way as the above examples, which are types of every-day drinking among average middle-class, commercial, and private individuals. When it comes to the case of the chronic drinker, who does his imbibing on the quiet, it is another matter. Drink, to him, is life — rapidly leading to death, it is true—and he could no more get on from day to day without his constant "nips" than he could fly. Many cases of this sort are hereditary, but there are to be found, in the seamy side of life, cases where men have been driven to drink by circumstances over which they had no control. Faithless wives, false friends, and the millstone of misfortune are all things calculated to drive a man to drink, and if the Elysium it provides be a fatal one, it is still to him, *pro tem.*, a respite from his sorrows, and dulls the powers of a wracking brain whose action brings back memories of the past, and heaps up shadows that he dare not face. There is no reformation for this class of drinkers, and when they end their miserable lives by suicide or any other means, their friends can only whisper a fervent "Amen," and pray to God to guard them from a similar fate.

There is no harm in drinking, providing it be done reasonably and rationally, and it is only when the alchoholic demon gets possession of men, body and soul, that it becomes a blot upon our civilisation.

DOMESTIC NUISANCES.

THERE are many kinds and orders of domestic nuisances—even excluding the domestic tabby (responsible for breakages and disappearances of an extraordinary kind), and the punctual and frequently unsatisfied collector of taxes. There is, for instance, a certain type of the domestic slavey who possesses an unique collection of original ideas eminently unsuited to her position in life. This kind of nuisance seems to have a notion that she ought to be allowed to solve, at her employer's expense, the problem of how to obtain the maximum amount of wages for the minimum amount of labour. She has also peculiar ideas as to the meaning of a specified hour (at which hour she has to relinquish her young man and return to the domicile where she breaks pots and retails her woes to her fellow slaveys), and fondly imagines that 9 P.M. means 9.30, and 10 o'clock as near 10.45 as she can with any degree of safety make it.

But it is not of the nuisances of the kitchen or basement that I desire to speak. It is of the recreative or drawing-room types that I wish to discourse. They are the *bête noir* of people who are so placed in life that they pass a certain portion of their leisure time at "At Homes" and domestic evening parties. Like many other people in this vale of tears, they labour under the fond delusion that they are, like a certain well-known pen, "a boon and a blessing to men"—and women. But a painful experience has proved they are in error. They are the innocent cause of pain and suffering in the bosoms of their friends and enemies, who are occasionally driven to do rash things in consequence of their efforts.

Firstly, there is the amateur reciter, who will recite pieces that have been hacked to death by all sorts and conditions of elocutionists. This nuisance appears to think that people are not yet familiar with the fact that a certain young party of historic fame was blessed with the cognomen of Norval, and that his respected sire fed sheep upon the Grampian Hills. He also desires to impress on the minds of the limited public he appeals to, that one Horatius did deeds of daring in keeping at bay the Tuscan army "in the brave days of old." Now, as all schoolboys and children of a larger growth are as familiar with these facts as he is, I cannot help thinking that the reciting nuisance is, in addition to inflicting pain upon innocent people, wasting his time and energy by unnecessary reiteration of fact—or fiction. This nuisance is a curious example of the fact that the human anatomy is not at all times what it should be. He invariably has trouble with his hands and arms. He gets them into the most peculiar positions, and finally, after imitating the action of windmill sails, and indulging in other gesticulatory efforts of an equally peculiar kind, he dives his hands into his trousers pockets and lays the flattering unction to his soul that he has overcome the difficulty of being perfectly at ease. Poor deluded mortal, if he only knew how awkward he looks he would take a few elementary lessons in gesticulation and then cease reciting altogether. But he is not constructed in that manner. He believes he has a mission to fulfil, and he will proceed upon the uneven tenor of his elocutionary way without regard to the consequences either to himself or his hearers.

Then there is that terrible nuisance, the amateur tenor, who delights to announce vocally his admiration for a maiden rejoicing in the name of Sally and residing in a common or garden alley. I have long had my doubts as to the accuracy of Miss

Sarah's address, and have a notion that
the poet who sung her praises used an
alley for the purposes of rhyme only. Else,
why did he become so familiar and call the
lady Sally instead of Sarah. Might he not,
with more propriety, have written—

> Of all the girls that are so smart
> There's none like pretty Sarah,
> She is the darling of my heart,
> And no maid could be fairer.

This would at least have been more polite,
and would also have been a sort of pallia-
tion for the liberty taken in publishing
the lady's private address. But poets have
no sense of the ordinary fitness of things.

But to return to the domestic tenor.
Whatever the failings of domestic tenors
may be, no one can deny that their vocal
aims and desires are identical. There is a
similarity about them which is appalling.
They delight to sit at the threshold of
their sweethearts' chambers and sigh. They
all want their lady-loves to "come into the
garden," and they are one and all wildly

anxious to fall like soldiers (I wonder how a soldier really does fall?). Then again, they all have a message to send to a maiden, whom, strange to say, they all "loved best." Now, however laudable these aims and desires may be, one is apt to become tired of hearing of them when they are trotted out on every possible occasion. Domestic tenors are of various qualities, and the suffering inflicted by their efforts varies largely in accordance with the strength or weakness of their vocal powers. No amateur tenor is ever happy until he has a big top note, and when he gets it, so do all his friends until they are weary of it. That top note is usually fatal, and is the cause of the tenor's fall both musically and socially. After a more than usually severe dose of the tenor nuisance I have often yearned for another world, where the tenor did not warble and his hearers were at rest.

The patience of ordinary mortals is, in

the matter of aspiring artists, long-suffering, but when it comes to infant prodigies,
even the most forbearing people are apt to
rebel.   Infant prodigies are, without doubt,
the most terrible of the domestic nuisances,
they are exhibited whenever opportunity
occurs, and they attempt the most trying
feats of art in a manner which makes feeling folks tremble.   There is not an instrument invented that has any terror for the
infant prodigy.   From the pianoforte to the
violincello, from the cornet to the trombone
—all are alike to him.   He will try his
hand at anything, and I fully expect to
be asked out some evening for the purpose
of seeing some six-year-old infant emulate the
feats of Sandow or attempt to take down
the record of the last Italian fasting man.
A tax on prodigies would be a blessing.

A terrible nuisance is the old gentleman
who has a story to tell, but which, in spite
of the fact that he has been trying to tell it
regularly for the past fifteen years, he has

never completely finished. He laughs con-
sumedly at his own stories, thereby breaking the thread and spoiling what to him is
the point of his narrative. It is no use
trying to avoid him, for he is certain, like
Mephistopheles, to "have you" by-and-by.
He buttonholes you in a semi-confidential
way and whispers into your ear. He is
irrepressible, and as much to be avoided
as the Russian influenza.

Then there is the lady pianist, a domestic
nuisance guaranteed to drive anyone with
a musical taste completely mad in the
shortest possible space of time. Once
place her in front of the pianoforte,
and Tennyson's brook is, in the matter
of running on, a fool to her. She
plays with an utter disregard for consequences, and the number of correct notes
she plays in a piece is only equalled by
the number that she doesn't. She plays
Schumann and Chopin on the same lines,
and seems to take a fiendish delight in

rendering well-known compositions in such
a manner as to render them unrecognisable
to those previously familiar with them.
There are, I know, people who would consider this a praiseworthy ambition. The
composers of the pieces might, were they
asked, think otherwise. She plays with a
boarding-school style, and has about as much
music in her soul as the animal that ele-
vated the proverbial fiddler. There is
usually a hum of conversation going on
during her performance, which produces a
sigh of relief at its conclusion. Whether
these various domestic nuisances were
brought into the world to exact penance
from sinful mortals I have never yet been
able to ascertain. But there is no doubt
that an extensive acquaintance with them
conduces to a sadder state of mind, and
many people may, after a social evening,
be tempted to ask, "What have I done to
deserve this?"—a state of affairs not
unlikely to lead to penitential feeling.

LOVE.

LOVE has been precociously described as "an itching of the heart that you can't get at to scratch," and there might be a worse definition of the tantalising passion.

There is something about love which defies description, and it seems at times to revel in its very vagueness. It is the most cosmopolitan of all the passions, and has even less respect for persons than the law, with which it occasionally brings worthy people into close contact. The chawbacon of the country, who giggles and smiles all over his particularly open countenance when he comes across his "gurl," is affected in exactly the same way as the Johnnie who gets what he calls "awfully dead spoons dontcher know" on his last new feminine fancy. You can never calculate

on love, and the histories which pretend
to give the world some idea of the god of
love as personified by the young gentleman
with a plentiful supply of arrows and a
scarcity of apparel, one and all point to
the fact that he is a mischievous young
monkey who takes a savage delight in
thoroughly annoying mortals who cannot
"round" on him. Like a big favourite in
a horse race, he's always an "odds on"
chance. If the relative positions of the
parties concerned were put on record at
their proper rate of odds they would read
much as follows :—

THE MATRIMONIAL STAKES.

Cupid, by Mischief, out of Spite, 9 to 4 on.
Johnnie, by Mash, out of Mind, 2 to 1 against.
Claudine, by Dead Set, out of Engagement, evens.

The principal feature of love is its un-
reliability. You can never rely upon it;
and I venture to say that were Cupid to
set up an establishment for supplying
young men and maidens with love potions

or barbed arrows at the lowest possible cash terms, he would find himself in the bankruptcy court in a very short space of time.

He does not even condescend to give people time to get used to his vagaries, but being, as it were, on tour, he spots out some unoffending mortal, sends one of his arrows into his heart and, hey presto! the mortal straightway falls in love with some fair damsel whom in all probability he has never seen before, and whom he has as much chance of marrying as he has of flying to the moon. And Cupid thinks it is funny.

In the songs and ballads love is supposed to be a thing to yearn for, and if the things said of it were true there could not be found any single patent medicine to equal it. But these writers of love songs do not always tell the truth; they have so much of what they call "poetic licence" to go at, and if you begin to argue the point with them they trot out their licence (for which they do not pay any fee) and tell you you know nothing about love or the beauties of verse. The latter assertion, so far as their own productions go, is generally true.

Let us take a glance at the real way in which love takes hold of people as opposed to the teachings of the spring poets.

A young man meets a girl, say at a dance. He has never seen her before, but the moment that his eyes rest upon her pearl-powdered cheek (in the distance) he becomes aware that unless he can induce her to take a permanent interest in himself his life henceforth will be a blank. How he arrives at this decision is a thing which has never yet been solved; sufficient for the day, or night, is the evil thereof—he does!

Then he gets someone to introduce him to her and gets a freezingly polite bow as the result of his labours.

In the old ballads he would have gone down upon his knees and declared his burning passion upon the spot and upon the carpet. But here he only says a few common-place things about the weather and then leaves his lady-love. He goes home and dreams about her, and when he gets up he exhibits indifference as to the contents of the breakfast-table. At business he mixes up attempt at verse with commercial correspondence, and gets into trouble in consequence. Even this does not damp his ardour or his love.

He knows the lady's address and spends the evening lounging about in front of the house with a view to catching a glimpse of her through a window or of seeing her shadow on the blind. So long does he stay that the policeman on the beat at length takes a personal interest in him, and then he goes home thoroughly convinced that the lady is in love with him and that it only requires time, patience

c

and opportunity for him to win her. This kind of thing goes on until the lady marries some one else, when her silent admirer comes to the conclusion that he had been badly used and takes violently to liquid solace.

This is the reality of love, and the poets know nothing at all about it, take my word for it. The poets tell us that "love that slumbers dies." Now I venture to say that if love, in the form of male humanity, dared to slumber when in the presence of his inamorata he would be too busy to die, for the lady would wake him up to a proper sense of the obligations due from a lover.

Love, even in its purest form, is the most selfish of all the passions, and is productive of jealousy and other equally objectionable things.

The young man who is in love objects to the object of his passion being pleasant to any other Johnnie, and if the young

man himself happens to be agreeable to
anyone but his special girl he may look
out for squalls on the first convenient
opportunity. If by any chance *he* com-
plains about a modest flirtation he is told
that he is mean and selfish, yet should
he follow suit he is certain to be informed
that he is acting dishonourably and playing fast and loose with his lady-love's
affections.

Believe me, love is very pretty—in the
abstract and in the ballads—but in reality
it is an annoying and mischief-making
passion. In its earlier stages it leads to
spooning, thence to matrimony, and thence
to the divorce court. And yet people are
daily asking why bachelors are on the
increase? As if any sensible man would
go out of his way to become acquainted
with a passion calculated to upset his
plans, cause him sleepless nights, and
materially interfere with his digestion.

MEMORY.

MEMORY, broadly speaking, is a marvellous mystery of nature, and not even the cleverest scientists are able, definitely, to say of what it really consists. That we have what is called memory we all know, that there are many people who can remember well, while others remember badly, we are also aware, but what is the actual process of mental storage has never yet been accurately propounded.

Wonderful feats of memory are on record, and it is told of some men that they could read a whole column of a London daily paper through once, and then repeat it correctly. I have never yet come across such a man, and in spite of the belief of other people I decline to accept the feat as a fact. Actors frequently are compelled to study their parts very rapidly, but I never yet met one who would undertake to "collar" a column of newspaper type at one reading. I have had some considerable experience of mnemonics, and my own opinion is that the memory can be trained and by practice improved, but I should doubt it going so far as to perform such a feat.

Of aids to memory there are no end, but I do not think them of much value, as I imagine all they teach could be acquired by constant use of the memory. These aids are mostly diagrammatic and require the student to think of one thing for the purpose of remembering another. It is told of a professor of the art of mnemonics, that after he had lectured on the advantages of his system and proved that once you learned it you could not forget anything, he had to send a small boy to the lecture hall after he departed to say that he had forgotten his umbrella. *Verb sap.*

A form of memory that is most annoying is the "convenient" memory. Its
possessor has a happy, or unhappy, knack
of forgetting things he desires to ignore.
It is no use telling him how to improve his memory, he will conveniently
forget what you tell him, and when you
lend him an umbrella on a wet night, you
may be certain that if it rains the following day he will forget to return it. In
youth there is no phrase more familiar to
the ears than "Oh, I forgot." It is a
curious phrase, and may be generally
traced to two causes, the first of which
is a desire not to do a particular action,
and the second an absolute lapse of
memory. In either case the consequences
are usually unpleasant for all parties concerned. It is a common cry that husbands
are lacking in mnemonic power in reference
to domestic commissions, and "Oh, I forgot
all about it" is a common sentence in the
castle of domesticity.

Without memory a large percentage of life would be a blank, and much happiness would be lost to thinking men and women. To forget is sometimes a negative pleasure, to remember is often a perfect Elysium of silent joy. Memory is a convenient faculty and does not, as a rule, hamper itself with the unpleasant past, but only gathers into its fold those things which have been part and parcel of the happiest periods of departed time. As Mr Jerome happily says, " It is the brightness, not the darkness, that we see when we look back. The sunshine casts no shadows on the past. The road that we have traversed stretches very fair behind us. We do not see the sharp stones. We dwell but on the roses by the wayside, and the strong briars that stung us are, to our distant eyes, but gentle tendrils waving in the wind. God be thanked that it is so—that the ever-lengthening chain of memory has only pleasant links, and that the bitterness and sorrow of to-day are smiled at on the morrow."

Who is there that has not at some period of life enjoyed the luxury of an hour with memory, when childhood and youth have come back with all the reality of their pre-existence, and when the scenes and actions of departed years have passed in dioramic order through the cells of memory. Every pleasure of the past has its secret hiding-place in the mnemonic storehouse, whence it creeps slily out at unexpected moments to remind us of its presence and to bid us remember, perchance when life seems sad, that we have tasted its sweets as well as its bitters.

To some people the saddest memories are a pleasure, for even if the thoughts of departed loved ones are tinged with grief, they are ever surrounded by the remem-brances of the happiness we shared with them ere the old reaper gathered them into his fold and rowed them solemnly across the silent river. This is why God's Acre is tended with such care, and why the last resting-places of the departed dear ones are strewn with the floral emblems of purity and love.

Youth is full of sentimental memories, and even jilted maidens store up in the book and volume of their brains memories of the honied words so fondly spoken by their deceitful lovers.

True-hearted lovers live largely on the delights of memory. What girl who has been wooed, has not a well-filled treasure-house of memories? Each word, each action, during the happy days of love-making, are religiously preserved, and when circumstances prevent the usual evening meeting, memory comes to the rescue, and the lovers live over their last meeting; and, aided by the spur of memory, weave fond thoughts of love within their minds, which help to strengthen their affection and bring them solace for the disappointment resulting from their being temporarily parted.

Even the old folks are tinged with the fever of love memories, and many a tale of departed pleasure is recounted by Darby and Joan as they sit round the fire in the autumn of life and dream of the days that will never return.

AMATEUR TIPSTERS.

THERE are certain things in this world which are best avoided by the man who desires to live a peaceful and sober life, and to be free from those worries and anxieties which beset sorely - tried mortals in spite of their best endeavours to avoid them.

Amongst these are amateur tipsters and their tips.

There is no one who is so certain as a man who has a tip. He knows it will come off, and he tells all his friends to back it, though he occasionally has sense enough not to back it himself, which proves that there are times when a man's common sense overweighs his infatuation in spite of him-self—though it is perhaps fair to add that he frequently refrains from "having a bit

on" from the important fact that he is
minus the "bit" to have on.

There are many types of tipsters as there
are many kinds of tips (though variety in
the matter of tips is usually but poor consolation to the backer thereof), and I will
touch on the salient points of one or two
of them from the point of view of experience.

Firstly, there is the fatal tipster who
has got what he designates "a dead snip,"
and which invariably — so he says — has
come direct from the owner or trainer of
the horse he knows cannot lose the race he
tips it for. It has long been a mystery to
me why an owner or trainer should give
his "dead snips" to people who have no
connection with him, and whose interest
in the turf is limited to supplying accom-
modating bookmakers with their weekly
amount of loose cash, yclept "pocket
money." For I have noticed that the
purveyor of good things given him by

owners and trainers generally holds a
position in the world of commerce, the
salary attached to which could hardly be
considered fabulous. Yet he would give
you the impression that he was in the
secret of the great stables of the turf and
on familiar terms with half the leading
members of the Jockey Club. Where he
in reality gets his tips is a mystery, but
apparently he gets them with a regularity
that, if he backed them all, would speedily
land him in the Bankruptcy Court. But
as he never fails to trot out a "dead snip"
for every important race of the season, I
can only conclude that, for reasons best
known to himself, he does not. When he
does happen to back a winner he endeavours to convey the impression that
he has won a large stake (most likely a
modest half-crown would be his largest
stake on a race), but when he backs a
loser he never tells his friends of the fact,
but insinuates that he had a private hint,

also from an owner or trainer, at the last moment that his tip was being saved for something else.

Then there is the tipster who is lucky. He usually commences his career by investing a very modest stake on a horse he sees tipped in a sporting paper, which manages to get first past the post. He knows nothing at all about racing, but having a run of luck he at once poses as an authority on the turf and tells all his friends and acquaintances that he is "in the know," and can put them up to one or two good things now and then. By the time he has backed a few winners he has commenced to read all the sporting papers and blooms out as a tipster whose information is to be respected and relied upon. This tipster is not quite so dangerous as the man who claims acquaintance with owners and trainers, for he usually gets so mixed up by the legion of papers he reads that he at length has no definite opinion as to the winner of any particular race, but goes into details as to the chances of several candidates for each race and advises his friends to have a bit on "both ways," advice, which if followed out, hardly increases the belief of his friends in his ability as a tipster.

Another type of the amateur tipster is the man, usually middle-aged, who believes in form. Of all the army of amateur tipsters, he is the man most to be avoided. He never moves without *Form at a Glance* in his pocket, and I verily believe he attempts to increase his acumen by sleeping with the sacred and much-thumbed volume under his pillow. He can tell you the performances of almost any horse on the turf, and can point out on the publication of the weights for a handicap which horse ought to win on form, and whether any horse has not been fairly handicapped on its merits. To follow his tips it would be necessary to have a banking account of unlimited capacity, for it is one of his great ideas that if a horse has shown form it must be backed every time it runs. "It is sure to win in the long run," he argues, and in the "long run" backers of his tips are landed on to the verge of ruin, and find that when the vaunted good thing does come off that they have either got tired of backing it or are in such a financial condition that it is not convenient to put down the stake necessary to verify the tipster's opinion. There is one remarkable feature about this type of tipster—his firm and unshaken belief in his method of finding winners. In spite of reverses which would have disheartened most men, he sticks to his opinion that form is the keystone to turf success, and his only regret is that fortune has not enabled him to hold on long enough.

A terrible type of tipster is the man who is a distant relation of a jockey, and who gets his tips through the medium of the

jockey's father, cousin, or brother-in-law.
He always impresses on you the fact that
his information must be reliable, because
the jockey who sent it is his forty-first
cousin, three times removed (I wonder how
often a cousin can remove, and yet remain
a relation?) and that he is specially
engaged to ride the horse he sends, and he
says it can't lose. Yet it not unfrequently
does. The peculiarity of this man's tips
is that they are always the horses his far-
removed relative is engaged to ride, and
who seems to be imbued with a notion that
if he rides a horse it must win, a notion
which, I regret to say, experience has
rudely shattered, for his position in the list
of winning jockeys is very nearly at the end.

Now, I think there is a moral to be
deduced from these amateur tipsters and
their ways, and that is that it is one of the
strongest weaknesses (pardon the para-
doxical phrase) of the human constitution
for men to wish to pose as authorities on

D

something. All men, if they are worthy of the name, are possessed of a tinge of ambition and a wish to dispense information —more or less reliable—to their fellow-men. They like to feel that they are benefactors, and in their inmost souls the amateur tipsters are, I feel certain, fully convinced when they give you a tip that they are doing you a genuine service. They act with the most laudable motives, else why should they dispense their information—in perfect confidence and secrecy —to everybody they come across? This being the case, one can only regret the fatality which generally precludes their efforts from resulting in permanent pecuniary benefit to their friends and followers.

SHABBY GENTILITY.

THERE is no more tantalising state of
existence in this vale of tears and sorrow,
than that known to the world as the shabby-
genteel. Like the proverbial drop of water
on the rock it has a wearing effect, a
tendency to make men bitter and women
mean. The whole atmosphere surrounding
the kingdom of shabby-gentility is tinged
with cynicism and its inmates are apt to
degenerate into scoffers. They always find
what they call Fate against them; their
lives are one round of shadows, and it not
unfrequently happens that when the grim
old reaper calls for one of their fellows, the
careworn remnants of humanity he leaves
behind almost regret he had not called
for them and left their comrade.

Few outside the fringe of the shabby-genteel domain know the ways and manners of its people. They little think of the struggle life is to them—especially to those who in brighter scenes lived happier lives. There is no house in the semi-respectable back streets and bye-ways where shabby-gentility resides that has not a history encased within its doors. No need to leave the neighbourhood if you desire to hear a thrilling story or a sad romance. They are all here, ready to your hand, if only you can get their heroes and heroines to unfold them for you. But shabby gentility is proud, very proud. Close clasped within hearts that beat beneath its threadbare garments it keeps its secrets and full often takes them with it to its last home in the green churchyard, where sorrow sleepeth and life's shadows cease. Yet, there is some humour to be found in the midst of all the sadness, some eccentricity of character worthy the study of a Dickens or a Sims. There is, for instance,

the military type of shabby gentility who
once held a commission in **Her** Majesty's
army, and who, having retired from active
service and gone through a fortune left him
by a benevolent relative, has entered the
land of the shabby-genteel to eke out the
remainder of his days on the munificent
pension granted him by a not-too-grateful
country. He is a figure in his little world
and is familiarly known as "The Major."
He has lost his money, but he has preserved his style; and though his clothes
are not of the latest, yet there is a
certain air of aristocracy about them
that never fails to have its effect
upon the casual observer. "Once a
gentleman always a gentleman" is his
belief, and in spite all his reverses he has
never lost that undefinable something that
stamps a man of birth and breeding. He
may only be able to wear the simplest
flower in his closely-buttoned frock coat,
but he wears it with all the distinction

with which he was wont to sport his
expensive button-holes in other days in
Regent Street or Rotten Row. The damsel
who supplies him with his morning bitter
at the hotel he frequents prizes more a
simple pansy from his button-hole than she
does the expensive roses brought her by
her wealthy but plebeian admirers. Yet
he is shabby-genteel, and he feels his
position acutely when by accident an old
friend passes him by with the stoniest of
smiles and the slightest inclination of a
wealthy head. He is considered a real good
sort of fellow by those who meet him in
the evening at the aforesaid hostelry, where
he tells tales of the world he once knew over
the cup that both cheers and also inebriates.
He can crack a joke with the best of them,
and when the laughter rings out loud and
long, little know his chorus of the memories
gnawing at his heart-strings, or of the black
ghosts of the dead past that rise to greet
him in his back room on his return to the

place he has of necessity made his home. They are not shabby-genteel.

Then there is the neat-figured young lady who goes out about half-past eight in the morning and returns within measurable distance of six in the evening. She has seen better days, and is now employed in the not too congenial occupations attached to the office of a daily governess. Her pallid face, gradually decaying garments, and sad smile tell of the wear and tear of shabby-gentility. She was wont—and that not many years ago—to dwell in the halls of dazzling light and to receive the flattery and adulation of the wealthy and the aristocratic. Speculation, reckless expenditure, and over-reaching after position in the world of society ended in ruin and disgrace, and the once-adored darling of the country side found herself reduced to the necessity of earning her own living in a world which has a contempt for shabby-genteel people. Her life is one daily round of drudgery, of trying to cram her stock of knowledge into minds not noted for their powers of receptivity, and of bearing patiently the impertinences and insults of her precocious pupils who, being the children of middle-class opulence, are not lacking in middle-class arrogance, and look upon a governess as a being two or three degrees removed from a housemaid or a gardener. Small wonder if the girl, after a long round of such drudgery as this, falls a victim to the pleading of some good-looking scoundrel, and leaves the haunts of shabby-gentility for what to her looks like a dream of bliss, but which, alas! too often turns out to be a reality of degradation.

Another type of the shabby-genteel is the white-haired lawyer's clerk, who has struggled for years for position and peace, but who is as near his goal to-day as he was thirty years ago. He is not unlike the lawyers one sees on the stage; staid, respectable and poor—very poor. He has

a regular salary and is in the employ of a
firm of some note in the world. But his
salary is not a large one, and he is expected to keep up a decent appearance in
the interest of his employers, who never
think for a moment that the salary they
pay him must, to a man with a wife and
family, mean an existence and not a living.
He is one of those unfortunate people
who are too useful to make any mark in
the world. Anything in the ordinary
routine work of his office he can do, and
it is his misfortune to have it to do
on any occasion when there is a push of
business. He has grown up in the dingy
old office where he went as a youth, and
has pottered on in regulation fashion while
less able but more spasmodically brilliant
juniors were promoted over his head. No
one ever appeared to think of him being
promoted—the place would not seem the
same if he were removed from his position,
and when he once asked for a change his

employers laughed and said he was too useful where he was and they really could not
think of such a thing. And so he went
on vegetating, earning the respect and confidence of all about him; but getting no
nearer the top of the tree than he was the
first day he mounted the stool he will in
all probability occupy until he dies. He
has grown so used to shabby-gentility now
that he would feel ill at ease if he were
suddenly removed to a sphere where
pinching and scraping to make ends meet
did not form part and parcel of his daily
life. There is not much difference in the
lives of those who live in this world I write
of. They are all occupied with the same
object—the terrible attempt to make their
neighbours think they are not what they
are. They tend with care their garments
and their secrets, and try to hide both
from the light of day. They do not live,
they only exist, and few, if any, of those
without the pale know what an awful heart-

aching business such existing is. Therefore, I say to those who are well favoured by Dame Fortune, do not sneer at the shabby-genteel, but lend them a helping hand when occasion offers, and believe me, you will get more satisfaction out of the action than you are ever likely to obtain from the usual sneer, which has an effect you do not wot of upon the lives of these poor unfortunates.

THE DRAMA OF LEGS.

IT has long been the firm opinion of certain actors, who spend many weary months of the year resting, that the British drama is slowly but surely going to the dogs. Which dogs are to be the recipient of the histrionic property I have not yet been able to discover. These actors (and their name is legion) will tell you, in the strict confidence begotten of a soothing beverage of. a spirituous nature, that in *their day* the stage was worth calling a stage, and the work *they* did was a credit and an ornament to the profession they condescended to adorn.

These grumblers belong to the heavy school of acting favoured by our fathers and grandfathers, who took their drama seriously, and could compare the relative methods of one actor with another with a critical acumen

not known to the ordinary playgoers of the
present day. Actors in those days were on
familiar terms with their auditors, and were
wont to discuss with them in convivial
fashion the merits and demerits of their
various performances. And in the old
stock days the actor's vocation was a varied
one. In those hard-working times the public
was regularly treated to what a modern
versifier calls

"The real legitimate and Billy Shakespeare's plays,"

and verily each player in his season played
many parts.

Whether these ancient Thespians were
accurate in their canine prognostication is
a matter for longer debate than my present
space permits; but it is an undeniable fact
that the form and fashion of the English
drama has undergone a material change
since the old days of stock companies. In
the old times pantomime was a thing
written and produced with some respect to

juvenile auditors, and was looked forward
to from season to season. A book was
written and people—actors and actresses—
were engaged to play it. The Merry Clown
and his welcome "Here we are again" were
greeted with genuine laughter by young
and old alike, and the story preceding his
antics was of a rational character. Nowa-
days his occupation's gone; his fooling is
done by "speciality" people in the opening, and he finds himself doing a fifteen
minutes' harlequinade to a beggarly array
of empty benches. People to-day who are
engaged to appear in pantomimes virtually
have a book written to play them.

And the drama? That has changed also.
In place of the plays our fathers watched
with interest we are presented with comedy-
drama, (why not tragedy-farce as well?)
farcical comedy, comic opera, and burlesque.
And which takes the most money? Comic
opera and burlesque. And why? Because
the public live at such a rate in the nine-

teenth century that they have neither the time nor the inclination to take their dramatic fare seriously. To them the theatre is a place of amusement pure and simple. It is a place to rest in, a place where the worry of business may be cast to the winds, and the antidote of laughter obtained as a remedy for the bane of high-pressure. Fun and plenty of it is the motto of the average playgoer of to-day, and it is to this feeling for pleasure and amusement that the drama of legs owes the hold it has obtained upon the playgoing public. The modern frequenter of the theatre does not care to think, and as serious drama, and even so-called comedy drama, requires some mental effort on the part of the spectator, it is always launched upon the sea of public opinion with much uncertainty. Plays, which to earnest students of the stage contain strength and beauty, have failed to attract the public, and have after a brief existence

been relegated to oblivion. The few pieces
of serious interest that have really suc-
ceeded of late years have owed much of
their success to the individual efforts of a
particular actor. In serious drama at the
present day it is frequently the actor or
actress who makes the play, and not the
author. Your stage-managing actor is a sore
destroyer of your author's lines and theories.

And the drama of legs—what is it? It
consists, broadly speaking, of two parts—
comic opera and burlesque. The former is
of several grades, and, with the exception
of the admirable nonsense written by Mr
W. S. Gilbert, it is principally noticeable
for the baldness of its dialogue, the
insanity of its lyrics, and the want of
originality in its plots. The latter consists
of an *olla podrida* of nonsense, jokes,
comic songs, dances and gags, and an unlimited display of the human form divine
on the part of principals and chorus in
tights and trunks. No one ever expects

rationality in a modern burlesque, and providing the leading lady—usually cast for the leading boy—is possessed of a neat figure, a pretty face and the semblance of a voice, she is as likely to pile up a fortune as a Nitrate King or a popular jockey. In addition to this, she may marry a duke — and probably live un-happily ever afterwards. Dukes and Earls are particularly partial to the drama of legs and its exponents. Whether we owe the drama of legs to the modern comedian —a distinct type from the comedian of the past—or whether the comedian to the drama of legs I am not prepared to state; but it is a certainty that in connection with the form of dramatic art in question there has risen up a school of comedians whose efforts lie solely in the direction of personal eccentricity. So far does this culture of personal peculiarities go in the drama of legs, that parts and pieces are specially put together for the purpose of

allowing an eccentric comedian to go on
and play himself, as it were. The amount
of mental effort and study saved to the
comedian by this phase of the drama of
legs must be enormous. No manager interested in the drama of legs can hope to
succeed without a chorus of damsels willing
to wear the garments — often limited in
quantity—of burlesque. Students of anatomy find the theatre a pleasant place
wherein to combine study of the human
form and recreation, for not even the most
carping critic can accuse the modern leg
drama pioneers of restricting their artistes
in the direction of anatomical display. They
are peculiar people are these chorus sup-
ports of the drama of legs, and live in a
world entirely their own. They are capable
of looking more inanimate than anything on
earth, and the regularity with which they all
do the same things in identically the same
manner is positively astounding. There is
nothing like it out of the drama of legs.

Yet they live and flourish, and are to be found on the stage of our theatres during the largest proportion of the dramatic year.

The producers — one can hardly say authors—of the drama of legs all work on the same lines. They give a catchy title to their work, such as "Guy Fawkes," "Lancelot the Lovely," and "Little Doctor Faust," which names serve to indicate that the piece has some slight connection with the subject its title parodies or burlesques.

Those who seek for a story in this form of the drama of legs will be woefully disappointed. It is not considered a necessity. Besides, it might interfere with the vagaries of the comedians, who, if they had to preserve it, would not be able to gag *ad libitum*, and that would be fatal in a drama of legs. To misquote the poet,

"Pieces come, and pieces go,
But gags go on forever."

No one is sacred; they use the names and

peculiarities of our greatest men for the
purpose of ridiculing them before the public,
and of gaining cheap applause at their
expense.   It is indeed a disgrace to the
playgoers of to-day that such should be the
state of affairs, but so it is.

Therefore, it seems to me that those
people who tell us that the stage is in a
better state than it was in the days of our
fathers are labouring under a sad delusion.
The social status of the actor may be a
better one than in the times when he was
dubbed a rogue and vagabond by Act of
Parliament, but that I fancy is largely due
to the Socialistic tendency of the age.
Amusement and not education is the cry
from all sides of the theatre, and until the
world moves at a slower rate, it will continue to be so. The drama of legs feasts
the eyes, pleases the ears, and supplies
sensuous idleness and real weariness with
pleasant sensations — hence its tremendous
hold upon the public. It is no use preach-

ing against it; there it is, a necessary evil of the times, and there it will remain until a radical change comes over the play-going community.

DOMESTIC MUSIC.

PERHAPS the most pernicious and demoralising of the recreations of this, our Island of England, is that terrible bugbear known as domestic music. I verily believe it is responsible for more sin and inquity than any other form of English entertainment. Lying, hypocrisy, and doubly - concentrated deception are one and all accentuated by the influence of domestic music. It has caused husbands to deceive their wives and families, and in his *Kreutzer Sonata* Tolstoi tells with terrible force how a wife used it as a blind for the purpose of humbugging her husband. But without attempting to treat the subject with the severity of the Russian novelist, who considers that music may rise to "the height of indecency," I propose to show some of the results accruing from indulgence in domestic music. I have frequently wondered whether Mr Gilbert had been the victim of domestic music shortly before he wrote the " Mikado ? " Surely so ; else he would never have perpetrated the keen and cutting satire of making his heroine fall in love with an amateur first trombone who, on his own confession, was "no musician."

In no place is the demoralising tendency of domestic music more *en evidence* than in the drawing-rooms of the middle - class communities. During the miseries of that essentially English institution, an evening at home, music is always more or less to to be found in the programme. And what is the result?

Lying! Sugar-coated lying perhaps, but none the less lying.

Let us diagnose the case and unearth the reasons for cause and effect. We will commence with the young gentleman who is labouring under the delusion that he is the possessor of a tenor voice. He is asked out so that he may experiment upon old-time songs, and new fangled waltz - re-frained ballads of love and sentiment.

He is fully aware of the prevalent fallacy as to his vocal powers, and gives himself airs only equalled in their absurdity by some of the so-called music he is so fond of warbling. As soon as things get into something like order in the drawing-room, he is asked to sing something.

He has been sitting in a corner of the room for some time, waiting for the moment when he shall be asked to perform, and is bursting with an ambition to show what he can do. He has brought a roll of music with him, and has carefully left it on the hall table. This gives him the opportunity of leaving the room to fetch his songs, and thus draw people's special attention to the fact that he is going to sing.

Yet when the hostess requests him to favour them with " one of your charming ballads, Mr Thomson," he feigns a well-studied hesitation, and remarks that "he would much rather not."

Of course he is pressed to oblige, and after some humming and hawing he consents.

This is the first phase of the hypocrisy resulting from Mr Thomson's vocal possession. The second follows—and it is the worse of the two — when he has tried to sing a song and has so distorted it that the composer would fail to recognise it.

The hostess tells him that his singing is "really charming," the young ladies call it "lovely," and his rival, the baritone, who hates tenors in general, and Thomson in particular, perjures himself by giving it as his opinion that he has "a very fine voice."

And all the outcome of domestic music. Very shocking it is to feel that what should be a harmless form of amusement produces such lamentable results.

Many a peaceful and respectable house-holder has, ere this, had cause to regret the existence of domestic music.

For instance, a nice, quiet old gentleman of studious habits may find his next-door neighbour has a passion for the cornet. This being so, the old gentleman is likely to be driven frantic by the efforts of his neighbour to perfect himself as a cornet soloist. He practises all the evening and rises early in the morning to resume his studies. It can therefore be no matter for surprise if the studious one indulges in strong, not to say profane, language. And should he be tempted to transgress the rules of sobriety occasionally, it can scarcely be wondered at. An amateur who is trying to play the cornet is calculated to drive any rational member of society to the verge of distraction.

There is but one way to settle such a man, and that is to employ a man who knows nothing at all about music to take the house next door and perpetually practise on the trombone.

Yet the man and his torment are simply the result of domestic music. He is anxious to appear before his friends as an instrumentalist. Poor mortal, poor friends. The old lady, who told her son to "put his fiddle away until he had learned to play it," had, in spite of her Hibernian blunder, much method in her madness. She knew perfectly well that the preparation for the production of domestic music is as likely as not to lead to fatal results—moral or physical.

I am told, upon the authority of a teacher of the instrument, that the flute is becoming a popular and fashionable instrument with the fair sex, and ere long the lady flautist will be included on all occasions when domestic music is to the fore. I regret to hear it, for next to the man who plays upon the cornet I should place in the category of musical nuisances

the lady who plays upon the flute. Yet
there is much sin and wickedness in the
world, and domestic music, and especially
female flautists, may be a form of penance
designed by a long-suffering Providence.
If the pain inflicted be equivalent to the
sins committed by performers and listeners,
the remedy will, indeed, be a drastic one.

The lady pianist is on the same level
with the tenor, the only difference being
that her sex entitles her to be the recipient
of more perversions of the truth in the form
of compliments than the male pretender.

Seriously, domestic music is undermining
the moral nature of the young people who
indulge in it. They say things about each
other that they do not mean and know to
be untrue, and their only excuse is that
the truth is not pleasant at all times, and
that they must be civil to the people they
meet at their own and other people's houses.

And all this is the outcome of domestic
music.

PICTORIAL ADVERTISEMENTS.

Mr William Tirebuck, of *Dorrie* fame, once sent out a circular announcing a lecture, entitled "Blank Walls," and I doubt not that he would draw, in his own peculiar and fanciful style, a graphic picture of the disadvantages, from an intellectual point of view, arising therefrom. No one knows better than Mr Tirebuck the pleasures missed by the possessors of blank walls.

Professor Herkomer years ago went further than the domestic regions touched upon by Mr Tirebuck, and turned his serious attention to the hoardings of the highways and bye-ways of large towns, and tried, in vain, to inculcate in the minds of those responsible for the adornment of the posting stations the lesson that wall - posters should be treated in the same way as a picture on the artist's easel.

He drew a poster in the Greek fashion, but as it related to nothing in particular it failed to attract the attention of the commercial advertisers, who consider that any artistic merit in a poster is a waste of time if it does not throw into relief the particular virtues of the article they desire to sell.

"Sweet are the uses of advertisement," said a well-known scribe, and he spoke with knowledge and accuracy. Advertisements bring before the public notice the value of many things they want and many things they do not want.

If a man desires to furnish his house when on the eve of matrimony, he has but to turn up the pages of a magazine or cast his eye over the first hoarding he passes, and he will find advertisements of how to furnish a cottage or a mansion, with illustrations of how the mansion will look

when furnished, not forgetting sketches of
the people who are likely to be in it, and
who always appear to me as though they
were having an intensely uncomfortable
time of it. It is, however, seldom that
he is supplied with a sketch of the cottage
"furnished completely" (or incompletely)
for five pounds. It is a *sine qua non* in
designing pictorial posters that nothing
shall be shown which is not attractive.

There are many lessons to be learned
from the contents of the hoardings and
from sources one would little dream of.
For instance, the hoardings have long impressed upon the public the importance of
asking for Glenfield's starch and seeing that
they got it. "*See that you get it.*" Do
not be put off with worthless imitations
but see that you get it. What a lesson in
firmness may be learned from these simple
words placed beneath the flaming picture
of a box of the well-known starch. Do not
be weak - minded—do not be deceived by

the bland persuasion of the enterprising
tradesman with a desire to palm off an
inferior article at an extra profit. No, be
advised by the poster, and, asserting your
manliness, "see that you get it." You
will then be able to go home with the
conscious feeling that you have defended
your rights, and when your shirts and
collars are washed and ironed you will not
be able to grumble because they are not
stiff enough for your fastidious taste. This
will probably lead to a lesson in forbear-
ance; and if you be an honest man, you
will feel that the pictorial poster is capable
of producing results not thought of by a
casual observer.

No article of commerce has had more
pictorial attention paid to it than soap.
Even artists of repute have turned their
serious attention to the cleansing necessity, and
poets have been laid under contribution for the
purpose of testifying to the virtues of a particular make which is publicly stated to be

"matchless for the hands and complexion."
"The Nightingale, the Lily and the Rose"
have united to sing its praises, and I once
saw a drawing of a dirty-looking individual
who had written to the makers, "I used
your soap ten years ago and I have used
none other since." His appearance bore
witness to the veracity of his testimonial.

From pictorial advertisements connected
with this soap one may get a pretty
definite idea of infantile happiness. A
child in its bath has lost a cake of this
soap, and it is announced that "he won't
be happy till he gets it," and on a
companion picture where it is shown that
the child has recovered the lost tablet it
states "he's happy now." What a con-
crete summary of life, and all from a soap-
maker's pictorial advertisement. All men
are unhappy when they see anything they
prize, and their sum of happiness is not
complete until they gain or recover the
things they desire. Judging from the

F

specimens of beauty depicted on the pictures as resulting from the use of this soap, it appears to me that it only requires a constant use of the commodity to ensure universal loveliness throughout the length and breadth of the land.

Other soaps there are for which equal merit is claimed, and one brand I have noted, the advertisement of which, with conspicuous honesty, states that it "will not wash clothes." There is something surprising in the fact of there being anything modern soap cannot do. In fact, I have often wondered it was not announced that the latest invention in soaps would cure all the ills that flesh is heir to.

But that is, not unnaturally, left for the pills and patent medicines to accomplish Wonderful things these.

> If half they say upon the walls
> About the pills were true,
> All folks would be so jolly well
> They'd not know what to do.

In fact, if all the posters state were even partially carried out there would be no work left for the doctors, and the vendors of pills would have to retire from the fact that nobody was ill. In this direction all the pictures are those of people who, having taken patent pills and medicines, have been restored from the brink of the grave to the height of good health.

The one striking thing about the pictorial and other advertisements of these patent healing preparations is their modesty. Here is a specimen of one of them.

"Camomile Pills, the most certain preserver of health, a mild, yet speedy, safe and effectual aid in cases of indigestion and all stomach complaints, and, as a natural consequence, a purifier of the blood and sweetener of the whole system."

Now, what could be nicer than the above. You are out of sorts, you take a dose of these pills and at once your whole system is sweetened, and you feel a new man.

People who pass a hoarding with its scores of pictorial advertisements and note not with care its varied announcements do not know the lessons they are missing, and the boons and blessings, from patent pens to electric belts, they are allowing to pass unnoticed.

Attraction is the watchword of the modern advertiser, and it is to the craze for distinction that the development of pictorial advertisement is due. Thousands of pounds are yearly spent on it, and if young artists would turn their attention to pictorial posters, and fling to the winds tall notions about Art (with a capital A), when they are barely existing by the production of pot-boilers, they would be able to live in comfort, and gradually improve their art work in their leisure time. To those who turn up their noses at the notion—if any such there be to-day — it will be interesting to know that one of England's greatest artists kept his family during the early days of his career by producing carpet designs, while during the intervals of his labour he worked at his pictures, which he could not sell then, but which were destined to take the world by storm in later years. Pictorial advertisement taken seriously is a phase of the age in which we live, and shows that the producers of soaps, pills, and other commodities are prepared to encourage art productions when they are suited to their purposes. If this only resulted in pleased senses through the medium of the street hoardings, it would convey a boon on thousands whose eyes are rested by the pictures; but it would do more than that—it would train the eyes and minds of the uneducated to appreciate beauty and colour.

BREACH OF PROMISE.

THE individual who described marriage as woman's triumph over man might with equal truth have given the same definition to an action for breach of promise, for even if a woman fails to get the substantial damages she invariably sues for, it is a triumph for her to feel that she has avenged herself on her treacherous lover and shown the world generally and the jury in particular what nonsense some men can write when under the influence of the god of love. Actions for breach of promise arise from various causes, but generally with but one object—cash. It may, I think, be taken as correct that no woman who has any respect for herself or real affection for her lover ever figures in a court of law as a wronged and jilted maiden.

No, the woman who, metaphorically, lays bare her bosom and places her lacerated heart on view is not of a nature to feel much affection of any kind, and as for the pure and honest love that brings sunshine into the mansion and the cottage, it is a thing totally unknown to her. One of the principal reasons why women reduce their affection to the level of pounds, shillings and pence is that they desire to "take it out" of the man who has, in their opinion and in that of their friends, fooled them. As a matter of fact, they look upon the affair as a matter of wasted time which they think should be paid for at the highest possible rate. It is one of the peculiar weaknesses of a woman's nature that she does not take her reverses (if one can call the loss of a fickle lover a reverse) rationally. Women always go to extremes, and a woman who has had her affections trifled with, either pines away and dies prematurely, declines all future chances of matrimony, or sues her lover for breach of promise. There is no relying on women, in such cases as these. They are too erratic. One of the worst types of plaintiff is the lady who is described in the papers as "a designing woman." She is a veritable female bird of prey, and lives only that she may make mankind feel to the full that women are necessary evils, and that some of them are more evil than necessary. This woman has all her powers of fascination under her finger and thumb, and can turn on her charms to order. She has studied men and their ways, and knows how to draw them into her net and how to keep them there (if they be desirable) when she gets them. She is a proof that humanity can be moulded to the will, and the passions of nature, so dwarfed and strangled that they almost cease to be actualities. She is a society hawk, and is ever on the look-out for victims to swoop down upon and devour. When she gets her victim into her toils he has to pay dearly before he can escape, and when she brings her action for breach of promise she lays her damages on thick, and it is a case of thousands or nothing. In court she uses her regulated charms to the full, and not unfrequently has more effect on the jury than the eminent Q.C. who is engaged to point out to the Court and the world that his client is a badly-used and wronged woman. This lady invariably wins her case, and frequently it is only a question of the amount she is to receive for having lured a man on to do something foolish under the influence of an amorous intoxication.

Another kind of plaintiff is the girl who is persuaded by her friends that she ought to make her lover pay for jilting her. She is usually from the country, and has been "keeping company" with one of the desirable lights of the countryside, who, probably finding the charms of some town lady more to his taste, leaves Phyllis to her fate, at which, personally, she would most likely not feel much hurt (they seem to have a philosophical way of looking at things in the country), but her friends feel it is their duty to see that she avenges her wrongs, and so an action is brought by the jilted but not-hurt damsel, who simpers in the witness-box and feels very uncomfortable all through the trial. At the conclusion of the case she gets small damages and makes an enemy of a man who respected her and would—when she married someone else—have stood as godfather to her children, and been a friend to both her husband and herself for life.

Then there is the actress plaintiff (who has been much to the fore of late years with success), who sues her refractory admirer with the full knowledge that if she does not get all she desires, pecuniarily, out of him, she is obtaining a magnificent advertisement, and that her salary is pretty certain to increase soon afterwards. I have known a lady rise from the position of chorus-girl to that of leading lady in a provincial company for no other reason than that she had been jilted by a sprig of the nobility. Hamlet was right, and the philosophy of his friend Horatio was a long way from including all the things in earth or heaven. I vow he never thought of such a transformation as I have just named resulting from a breach of promise action.

From the defendant's point of view the law is decidedly objectionable. It virtually means that a man may not change his mind on a vital question without the risk of having to pay dearly for it.

Many a man has married a woman he did not care for rather than parade his error before the world and have his correspondence made fun of by a barrister, who in the exercise of his profession has no heart and no respect for the feelings of others.

Custom has made it the rule for men not

to sue for breach of promise when a woman
throws them over, yet a woman who, taking advantage of an opportunity and a
man's weakness, lures him on to an offer
he regrets directly afterwards can sue him
for breach of promise if he decides to
rectify his folly and to save both the
woman and himself from being wrecked on
the troubled sea of matrimony.   If a man
does take the law into his own hands, and
tries to equalise things by suing the false
fair one who has changed her mind, he
generally succeeds in getting the smallest
damages possible, and is chaffed and laughed
at by his friends and acquaintances.   Yet,
if a woman is allowed to sue for breach
of promise (and, I ween, they are quite as
fickle as men), why in the name of fortune
should it be considered mean for a man
to do it?   Are not our affections as valuable as a woman's?   Yea, verily, they
are.

One of the amusing tribe of defendants is

the middle-aged or slightly decaying gentleman who has placed his hand and heart
at the disposal of the lady whose charms—
to put it mildly—are on the wane, and
who feels that she is not likely to have
many more chances of becoming the loving
spouse of a husband past his youth and
with a comfortable income. There is a
Bardell-*versus*-Pickwick sort of air about
these once-amorous fogies which makes one
feel that they ought to make it up and
settle down into middle-class domesticity.

The defendant with means usually admits
the case against him and engages expensive counsel to try and convince the
jury that the damsel who is suing him
has not suffered to any appreciable extent.
This defendant's affection is of the mercurial
order, for he invariably marries some one
else within a short time of his case being
settled.

Breach of promise actions appear to be
part of the wild oats of titled youths with

a leaning towards the stage and its beauties
—of the female species.

The most entertaining part of a breach
of promise action invariably arises from the
reading of letters —fatal evidence in these
cases. These epistles are interesting as
showing the number of adjectives it is
possible to get into one letter, and not
unfrequently they form a sermon on the
way in which the passion of love fades
and dies under given conditions. They
are wise in their generation who pen them
not. Whether a lady who sues a man
for breach of promise deserves our pity
is a much-debated question, as is the
question whether the law on the point
should be altered. The moral of the whole
thing is simple. Do not make a promise
if you don't mean to keep it, but if you
break it square things out of court.

FORGETFULNESS.

FORGETFULNESS is not of necessity the result of what is called "a bad memory," but far more frequently arises from pure carelessness or lacking in the matter of concentration. The boy with his head full of his games forgets things of graver import from the mere fact that the faculty of concentration is being entirely devoted to the less important object or occupation.

The lover forgets some small commission undertaken on behalf of his mother or sister because his thoughts are with his lady-love. And the business man, with his mind full of the details of his ventures, forgets to buy his wife some present he has promised her, with the result that there is, on his arrival at home, "a storm in a teacup," which is more annoying than enduring.

And all the outcome of forgetfulness.

As illustrating the peculiar results of forgetfulness, it is told of a *paterfamilias* that, on leaving a steam boat laden with packages, he was asked by the captain, "Who owns these three children?" Whereupon he remarked, "I knew I'd forgotten something."

It is recorded of an eminent scientist that he used to forget that he had eaten his meals, and it is a fact that a bridegroom once forgot to turn up at the church on the morning when he was to have changed single blessedness for matrimonial uncertainty. It has never yet been ascertained whether this strange lapse of memory was due to physical or moral causes, but the fact that the bridegroom was missing when inquired for, rather points to the latter than the former.

The gentlemen who "borrow" things and

do not return them owing to forgetfulness, are of a numerous and varied class, and include in their ranks the nimble-fingered purloiner of the silk pocket-handkerchief and the enterprising burglar who "borrows" anything that is not too hot or too heavy to remove. *He* invariably forgets to return the articles he purloins, unless caught in the act by his natural enemy—a policeman.

There are few things more forgotten in this world than books. They outrival umbrellas. Once lend a man a book and it is almost a certainty that you will see it no more.

There is something peculiar about books, and they produce a forgetfulness which is really extraordinary.

An *apropos* story comes into my mind. A man was spending the evening with a friend and was particularly struck with his collection of books, included in which were many rare copies and first editions. As he was taking his departure he picked a book

from the shelf and said to his friend, "By
the way, old man, you might lend me this
for a day or two." To which the host,
pointing to the contents of the book-case,
replied, "Not likely, my boy; *I borrowed
those.*"

It is one of the great essentials of a
true gentleman or lady that they never
forget the little things which go to make
life pleasant, and no one is ever likely to
have their feelings hurt by either one or
the other owing to an accidental reference
to some subject which is painful and which
they desire to forget.

To many people forgetfulness is indeed
a boon, and many a poor devil has committed suicide from the mere fact that his
organism was so finely wrought that he
could not stand the perpetual strain of
memory. To such a man, forgetfulness is
Heaven, and he would sooner have his mind
a blank than be endowed with the faculties
of thought and memory. He wants to

forget, and anything that makes him remember . the shadows and thorns of his
wretched existence is a thing to be
avoided.

Do you think the woman who has given
her heart's love to a scoundrel and had it
lacerated by his coward hand, wants to
remember the days when, with implicit
faith and perfect love, she fell from purity
to shame? No, rather the silent river with
its rushing tide than the perpetual memory
of such a past. It is the absence of the
power to forget which drives these deserted
and dishonoured women into the primrose
path where pleasure's cup helps to drown
memory and guides them to a haven of
forgetfulness. Do you, good reader, never
feel that there are things in your life you
would like to pass into the region of
oblivion where thought and memory lie
dead, and where the ghosts of departed
days do not flit to and fro from hour to
hour with wan worn faces, which seem per-

petually to be saying "Do you remember?"
Conscience does indeed "make cowards of
us all," and it is when we feel its power
that we desire to forget.

It is no pleasure for the broken-down
man to remember the days when he
revelled in the delights of purple and
fine linen. No, he would rather forget
that he ever knew the pleasures attached
to them.

Apart from this phase, forgetfulness leads
to much unpleasantness, and I know of
no more pitiable object than the man of
forgetful habits, who, having tied a piece
of string round his finger to remind him to
"remember not to forget" something, has
to stand and ruminate because he has
entirely forgotten what it was he had to
remember. The last state of that man is
certainly worse than the first. Equally
absurd is the position of the man who
wakes up in the middle of the night with
the horrible thought that he has forgotten

to lock or bolt the door. He gets out of bed and shiveringly dons such of his apparel as will prevent his catching cold, and goes to remedy the accident. Arrived at the door he finds to his intense astonishment and annoyance that it is both locked and bolted. Then he returns to bed, making uncomplimentary remarks about himself as he ascends the stairs, but not even the satisfaction of knowing that he had not forgotten, repays him for the anger he feels at having had to get up because he fancied he had neglected the thing. As he drops off to sleep he mentally decides that in future the door may take care of itself; and if every door in the house is left open he will not get up to see to them.

As I said at the start, so I say at the finish—forgetfulness is the result of carelessness or want of concentration, and a little training in this direction would soon remedy all the evils resulting from it.

"Where are you going for your holidays?"
"Don't know; haven't quite decided yet."
This question and answer are, at certain
periods of the year, heard almost every day,
for it is at these times that people generally begin to wish for a change and feel a
desire for fresh fields and pastures new.
They want to get away from the humdrum
or exciting life they have led since their
last holiday, and to leave behind them
their cares and their business for such
length of time as circumstances permit.
They have come to the end of their
working tether, and want to enjoy the
delicious luxury of perfect idleness. There
are many people who have no idea of the
real delights to be obtained from a state of

dolce far niente. I once heard the head-master of a well - known grammar school say, in reply to a question as to his idea of a perfect holiday, that he liked nothing better than to "lie on his back and bask in the sunshine." And those who have in the summer-time tried the experiment will endorse his opinion. To lie at ease and dream away the hours in an absolute state of laziness is far more of a holiday than the regulation trips so popular with the masses, who, for the most part, know nothing of the Elysium of a "summer madness," which resolves itself into weaving fancies in the sunlight, and smoking the pipe of peace in an old and unweeded country garden, when the sun's sweet glow throws its rainbow tints on the surrounding landscape and glints on the spire of some old church whose very appearance and surroundings are redolent of peace and quietness. There is a delightful drowsiness about the very atmosphere, the birds seem to rest more frequently than elsewhere, and the bells pealing over the lea as the cattle plod their homeward way seem laden with suggestions of perpetual rest. But whatever difference of opinion may exist as to the best way to spend a holiday, there are few who do not share the belief that, to misquote the poet,

> There's nothing half so sweet in life
> As a fortnight's rest.

Let us take a brief survey of the manners and customs of the general run of humanity when it is out for its annual holiday. To begin at the beginning of the alphabet we find that the most caricatured and sneered-at holiday - makers are those residents of the great city popularly known as "'Arry and 'Arriet," who are generally supposed to revel in the delights of "'Appy 'Ampstead," or to find the perfection of enjoyment in a week at Margate. Whether they obtain rest from their stay at Margate or invigoration from "'Appy 'Ampstead" may be doubted, but that they obtain a certain kind of rough enjoyment is indisputable. As beauty is supposed to be dependent on the eyes of the beholder, so enjoyment is dependent on the constitution of the individual. What is enjoyment to 'Arry would be purgatory to the scholar. Young people, whilst drawing the line at the boisterous enjoyment of 'Arry and 'Arriet, generally like to make their holidays as lively as they can, and sea-side resorts are their favourite hunting-grounds. You find them in abundance at Bridlington, Blackpool and the Isle of Man. They go in for what they call fun, and do as much real hard work in a day as they do in a week at home. After the day's enjoyment is over they repair to the various boarding-houses and continue the fun inside with the result that they retire to rest tired out. I have known specimens of this type of holiday-maker go to a favourite haunt for a fortnight and then come home in such

a state as to necessitate a three weeks'
recuperating trip to some less lively district.
Yet were you to insinuate that they did
not know how to enjoy a holiday they
would laugh at you. If it be true that
change is rest they ought to be thoroughly
rested, for they not only get change of
scene but they entirely alter—for a fortnight—their lives and habits.

Aristocratic people choose their holiday
haunts according to the caprice of fashion,
one year perhaps going to Scarborough and
the next to Whitby, but wherever they
pitch their tents their *modus operandi* is
much the same.

They are seldom to be seen at any
resort that has not a saloon and a band,
for it is upon this regulation promenade
that they disport themselves morning and
evening. It is the saloon parade that
enables the daughters of society and their
maternal relatives to show off their holiday
frocks, hats, and sunshades to the delight

of themselves and the envy of their less fortunate sisters. This process is carried on morning and evening, the afternoons being generally devoted to sleeping or—very occasionally—driving. Society has an objection to turning out in the afternoon when away for its holiday. Sleep is necessary for the preservation of the good looks of the ladies—knocked up by a London season—and the male representatives find it "too much fag" to turn out. Thus they go the rounds day after day and pull themselves together for the remainder of the year, for holiday-making with Society is as often as not a process of repairing damaged constitutions. Those denizens of the world where the *crême de la crême* reside who go abroad when their friends stay at home are usually supposed to do so more from motives of economy than choice. A holiday to them is a necessity from other points of view than those of health and rest.

Paterfamilias, with a middle-class position and a sprinkling of olive branches, usually hies him with his belongings to some quiet, inexpensive seaside place where his youngsters can inhale an unlimited quantity of ozone, and where he can sit on the rocks and smoke while his better-half does needle-work or revels in the contents of a railway novel. These good people are not, as a rule, folks of many ideas, but they get more real value out of their annual vacation than the racketing youngsters or the Society swells.

Some sprinkling there has been of late from all the above types who have gone in for a big rush to the Norwegian fjiords, which they explore at the most rapid rate possible. They come back with marvellous stories of their experiences, and impress upon all their friends and acquaintances the vital importance of their starting for Norway at the earliest possible moment.

If you want hurrying out of your life

take their advice; if you want a rest, do not.

There are no people who appreciate and enjoy a holiday so thoroughly as the tired brain-workers. They know the value of rest to an extent undreamed of by the ordinary holiday-makers. They do not go off on frisky excursions, nor do they go to the latest fashionable resort of Society. No; they go to some quiet spot far from the madding crowd, and there amid pleasant and peaceful surroundings revive their worn-out energies. To them the country in its summer garments is a perfect paradise —the flowers have a sweeter odour than elsewhere, and the atmosphere seems filled with a sense of repose. They return to their labours (and there is no such tiring labour as brain-work) like giants refreshed, per-pared to do their utmost to enlighten or assist their fellows.

Now for a parting word to holiday-makers generally. If you want to get some meed of value from your holidays do not select a spot where the *genus* racketer is to be found.   His presence mars the prettiest of scenery, and his *modus operandi* is opposed to the rational method of taking a rest.

If you are thoroughly tired out, take my advice and select some quiet country village where the world you live in is a thing of hearsay only.   Nature unadulterated is the best remedy for overwork, and the versifier who said—

> " To the fields away ! for nature presses,
>   On toiling foreheads a balmy kiss.
>   There's nothing so sweet as her wild caresses,
>   No love more full to the lips than this,"

knew the value of rest and knew also where to find it.

INADEQUATE SALARIES.

THERE is but little doubt that a very large percentage of the workers in the lower strata of commercial England are underpaid.

Men are working long hours at starvation wages, and if they ask for an increase of salary they are told that no advance can be made in the rate of payment from the fact that plenty of men out of employment are quite ready to take their places at even a lower rate of remuneration than they are receiving.

This may be, and probably is, perfectly true, but it does not alter one iota the fact that inadequate salaries are paid by thriving firms to men whose labours they must know perfectly well are morally and commercially worth considerably more money than they are paying for them.

And this is not only the case in one special line of business, but, so far as those whose position is below that of a " head," is a general thing in all trades, and in not a few of the professions.

I venture to say that no small amount of the money amassed by some of the wealthy but plebeian pillars of commercial England has been made at the expense of men who were paid inadequate salaries.

The payment of salaries which are neither commensurate with the ability of position of the recipient must have, and has, a most demoralising effect upon those whose lot in life compels them to accept remuneration which they know full well is not what they should, in fairness and justice, receive for the work they are employed to perform. Let us take a glance at some of the fatal results accruing from the payment of inadequate salaries.

Take the case of a young man who is in the prime of life, and who has taken unto himself a wife, whose lot is cast in such conditions as her husband can provide for her.

The husband is employed in a good house of high standing in the world of commerce, and has, perhaps, worked himself up from a lowly position in that firm's office to the post of an ordinary desk-tied clerk, who does his monotonous routine work from nine o'clock in the morning until six o'clock in the evening. He is allowed one hour for his dinner, and if he be ten minutes late on his return from the frugal meal he is either severely frowned at by the head of his department, or is told in a manner highly suggestive of satire that he is not a punctual servant. He dare not reply to his superior officer, and has to grin and bear the rebuke with the inward thought that he has frequently to work long past the stipulated hours of his engagement, and that without either thanks or remuneration for his "overtime." For his work he is paid a miserable pittance, and his only excuse for saddling himself with a wife and the consequent domestic responsibilities is that he is certain to obtain a rise in position ere long. Fatal hope!

When he applies to his employers for an increase of salary on the double ground that he has been in their employ since he was a youth, and that he has a wife to keep, he is again frowned upon and treated to a lecture on the folly he has committed in letting his natural feelings get the better of his common sense. To this is added a few words as to the way in which the firm has raised him to the position he occupies, and it is very broadly hinted that "the honour" of connection with so highly-esteemed a house should be some recompense for the inadequate salary paid by the "highly-esteemed" house. So the clerk has to drudge on as best he can, and his wife and children have to bear the pain and degradation which are the salient features of life when it is a daily and weekly struggle to make ends meet.

I sometimes wonder if some of these commercial magnates ever think as they sit at their well-appointed tables with their dinners of many courses in front of them, what life must mean to the underlings whose ill-paid labour enables them to make their fortunes. I fancy not, or they would surely make some attempt to alleviate their sufferings. There are, however, worse cases to be found than that of the man with his wife and children dragging on a weary existence in a vain endeavour to keep up appearances. Many young men are not blessed with strength of will sufficient to resist the temptations of their daily life, and it is to these that inadequate salaries are more than ordinarily dangerous.

There is, and always has been, much outcry against gambling in general and among the youths of the country in particular. Many reasons have been assigned as the cause of it, and I wonder that no one has ever suggested inadequate salaries as one of the great reasons for, and incentives to, gambling, particularly in the direction of betting on horse-racing.

Let me explain.

A young man is in the receipt of small salary. He has friends and acquaintances whose financial status is, fortunately for them, better than his. They are able to enjoy the pleasures of life fully, are not compelled, as he is, to think twice before he spends once. To them a night's enjoyment or an extra drink or two are of no importance. To him they may mean pinching and scraping for a week or a fortnight.

Yet he is loth to give up the pleasure he loves so well, and can afford so ill. His friends or acquaintances are perchance of a sporting turn of mind, are lucky, and not unfrequently back a winner or two. All this is so easily done and seems such a pleasant way of adding to a limited income, that the ill-paid member of the clique begins to fancy he has only to back horses and he will straightway make a heap of money.

Acting on the advice of his friends, he puts a modest amount on a horse, and wins. From that moment he is a doomed man. Horse-racing is to him the high road to fame and fortune; his inadequate salary troubles him no longer, for has he not found a perpetual panacea for all his ills. But there comes a day when the horses he backs do not win, and he loses all he has made and more. He has gone so far that he cannot give it up, and even his limited income is used in the endeavour to retrieve himself. But ill luck lasts long, and he goes from bad to worse. At last he gets a big "tip" from a sporting acquaintance, who tells him it is *certain to win.* But he has no money to back the good thing with. Then comes the final fall. An open cash-drawer and an empty office offer opportunity, and with the certainty that he will be able to replace the money directly after the race, he helps himself to his employer's money. The horse loses, and he is discharged without a character, if he be not prosecuted for theft.

And all the outcome of an inadequate salary.

Had he been decently paid, the longing for unobtainable pleasure would have been checked, the temptation would have been avoided, and he would have been a respected member of society. And so it runs on through the world of commerce. Many ill-paid workmen are made to suffer and sin, while their masters are amassing fortunes with no care as to their servants' welfare.

GOING ON TO THE STAGE.

THERE is no trade, profession, or calling which the ordinary individual considers so easy to go into as that of the stage. Yet there is no calling in which the blanks are so numerous, the work so laborious, and the disappointments so tantalising.

Most people who contract a dose of what is known as "footlight fever" seem to be under the erroneous impression that even ordinary intelligence is on the stage, as in the proverbial government office, totally unnecessary. This is the first false notion that is usually impressed upon the mind of the embryo Henry Irving, or the would-be Sarah Bernhardt. These uninitiated aspiring Thespians fondly imagine that all they have to do to ensure a permanent entrance behind the scenes is to insert an advertisement in the *Era* or the *Stage*, stating that they are prepared to play a small part for an opening, and the rest is easy. Poor deluded mortals!

If they only knew — as they generally do, early enough — that the profession is crowded out with capable and experienced artistes, who are only too willing to work for the same salary they are prepared to supply high - class incompetency at, they would stick to their lasts — ay, even to shoemaking—with a satisfied mind, and not rush in where angels, if they lived on earth, would most assuredly fear to tread. It is no use beating about the bush in writing about the stage as a profession, and the sooner amateurs know that, unless they are especially gifted, have plenty of money, or immense influence, they are almost certain to fail, the better.

To succeed upon the stage it is a *sine qua non* that, in addition to peculiar talents, the aspirant must be capable of hard work, patience, and the necessary fortitude to face failure, snubs, jealousy, and its attendant spite, and the weary waits called "rests," that so frequently beset the actor in his way through the shoals and quicksands of the world of stage-land. People seem to have an idea that, to those stars they applaud at the various theatres they visit, life on the stage has always been as they see it. False notion, indeed, is this. Their position has only been gained by years and years of incessant toil and privation, and if they but told the world the true story of their fight, ere chance or influence placed them where they are, there would be less sunshine than shadow in it, I warrant.

No! The stage is a place to be avoided by those who are not more than usually adapted for it, and the percentage of these

is so infinitesimal in the ordinary walks of
life, that to ninety - nine out of every
hundred who propose to "go on to the
stage" it is perfectly safe to apply *Punch's*
advice to those about to marry—"Don't!"
"The glitter and glare of the road to
fame," as seen from the front, is all very
well in its way, but when the gilt is
removed from the theatrical gingerbread
there is very little left that is worth the
taking.

And to-day the state of things is, owing
to the society craze for the boards, worse
than ever it was, for the profession is
crammed with young swells and society
women, who, having enough money to live
on apart from anything they earn, can
afford to give their services to managers
free, in addition to using their influence on
his behalf, on such occasions as it may be
to his or their interests to do so. These
society mummers are the stage's worst
enemies, for in addition to adding to the

superabundance of mediocrity at present in the profession, they are taking the bread out of the mouths of men and women who have spent a lifetime in learning their business, and who are willing to supply a legitimate return for what I suppose, to be up to date, I must designate a "living wage." The proof of this is, that not only in London, but in one or two other towns, it is possible to pick up, at low salaries, a capable travelling company in practically a few hours. This being so, what chance has the ordinary inexperienced individual in the race of the stage? None. He has his trade to learn—the fact never enters his head—and he has to take his chance in a crowd where he is handicapped to the fullest extent ere he starts on the contest.

In no other competition would a man even dream of fighting against such odds. Yet such is the fascination of the stage, that men imbued with a fair education, and an average amount of common sense, throw

up decent positions to go upon a will-'o-
the-wisp hunt, that they must know they
have no earthly chance of being successful in.

Again, no, my would-be tragedy and
comedy merchants. Leave the stage to
those who are on it, and their name is
legion, and if you want any solace for your
wounded vanity, take a glance at the
Stage and *Era* every week, and add up
the number of talented people who are
" resting " or " disengaged " (it is usually
the same thing), and be thankful you are
not of their number, at the same time
remembering that they are but a tithe of
the poor men and women who are not
only " out," but who are, many of them,
on the verge of starvation and the workhouse.

The stage is not all bouquets, applause,
Johnnies, presents, and glorification, varied
by pink tights and diamonds. On the
contrary it is about as tiring a life as you

can find in a day's march, and the actor
who is revelling from the front in the
ringing applause of a crowded house, frequently acts with an aching heart and a
heap of memories of the "might have
been," which are sufficiently weighty to
have taken all the sunshine from his life,
and make him care but little for a success
that came too late, and the knowledge
which is only made the more bitter when
he goes home from the playhouse and
knows that the woman who shared his
privations is not there to enjoy his success.

These may seem pessimistic views to
take of a most popular profession, but
I am writing warning words which I
know are true, and I write as much
in the interest of the actors as the
amateurs.

Let the latter rest contented with their
lot, and if they want to air their Thespian
fancies, let them restrict their efforts to
amateur theatricals, where charity covers a

multitude of bad acting, and confine their stage proclivities to taking advice and hints from professional exponents of an art that is as difficult as it is admirable.

BACKING HORSES.

WHEN a hot favourite for a big race gets
beaten by a stable companion that stands
at a longer price, it is usual for backers of
the short-priced gee gee to decry the
turf, and to designate racing as the most
gigantic swindle on the surface of the
Almighty's universe. That there is some
truth in their assertion I am bound, from
experience, to admit, for the annals of the
turf in recent years have furnished specimens of refined and well-planned roguery,
which were worthy the brains of a Balfour
or the daring of an east-end London
burglar. Yet in spite of this common
knowledge the ordinary backer — *i.e.* the
genus punter—still pursues the even tenor
of his way with a persistence worthy of a
better cause, and a recklessness that would

do credit to a Beresford or a Stanley. He knows perfectly well in his better senses that he "didn't ought to," but he does.

The persistent punter has as much chance of making money at the game as he has of stopping waves with a pitch-fork.

The methods he uses to attain his ends are unique in their imbecility, and no sane man would dream of applying them to any ordinary business transaction, the ultimate aim of which was the making of that necessary evil—money.

Perhaps the principal and most extraordinary characteristic of the ordinary backer is the way in which he allows other people to rule and change the vacuum that he calls his mind.

He is always getting a straight tip—direct from the stable, my boy—but valuable and reliable as his information is supposed to be, he is invariably persuaded by someone else to back another horse. There is one thing that the punter is always to be relied on for, and that is, the way in which he can tell you what ought to have won on form. He is a walking encyclopædia of form, and invariably carries the latest edition of McCall in his pocket. Another of his strong points is his knowledge—after the race—of the fact that winners of big handicaps have been especially kept for them. In spite of which knowledge he generally fails to back them.

And now for a glance at his methods.

He is usually blessed with a firm belief in the opinions and advice of the sporting writer of one particular paper, and tells you with an air of superiority that he knows for a fact that he is paid an enormous salary, and in a moment of confidence imparts the information that he knows who he is. This is done to impress you with his, the punter's, standing in the world of sport.

He backs the tips of his pet until he finds that he is likely to arrive early in the

land of "brokedown," and then, taking the
advice of another of his tribe, flies for aid
to the tipster of some other paper who has
chanced to have a run of luck.

Frequently he is a subscriber to the
papers and telegrams of an advertising
tipster, and so long as he is doing well,
swears by him, leaving him like he did the
sporting writers, when his luck changes.

He has not even the courage of his
opinions, and if his first love comes back to
form and sends a lot of winners, he curses
his folly for not having stuck to him all
through.

He follows particular horses in the same
way, and after having preached them
during the whole time they were losing,
fails, principally from want of funds, to
back them when they romp home at remunerative odds, backed only by the connections
of the stable in which they are trained.
Ah! my poor deluded backer, you are,
in the words of that pathetic ballad—"At

Trinity Church I met my doom," the M. U. G.

You have no earthly chance; for the little backer, with the rarest exceptions, gets beaten in the end.

To paraphrase the words of young Laertes when he slanged the Sky Pilot who refused to say the burial service over his sister, Ophelia, when she suicided :—

> I tell thee, foolish backer,
> A man of fortune shall thy " bookie" be,
> When thou'rt stone broken.

In writing thus, I am perfectly aware that general gambling will never be put down by Act of Parliament, nor will betting on the turf, for if the latter were dispensed with there is but little doubt that the turf, as it is at present constituted, would cease to exist. And so long as the powers that be in the land are allowed to have their thousands on, I fail to see why the punter should not have his half-crown on also.

But the main points of my article remain the same. The punter will probably reply that the big backers make it pay, and why shouldn't he? Allowing that the big backers do—which, with one or two exceptions, I doubt considerably—they are in a better position to get at the way the wind is blowing than are the entire army of punters combined. And even then we hear of big owners retiring in disgust, either from the fact that their horses have been run on the cross without their knowledge, or that they have failed to make racing a financial success.

All the plungers of late years have gone under, and the warnings off within easy remembrance rise up in the mind with the blackest surroundings.

These are facts that the ordinary punter should ponder over.

I would not, for a moment, deprive any man of the pleasure of a casual bet, but, it is the fact that he does not stop there

that ruins him. Trying to get it back is
the bugbear of the punter, and the opportunity of the bookmaker.

As showing what chance the punter who
relies upon advertising tipsters has, the
following remarks of the Duke of Portland
are interesting :—" There is no doubt that
many young people are tempted to bet by
the glowing advertisements they see in
certain of the daily sporting papers. Well,
gentlemen, I would take this opportunity
of warning them, from my own personal
experience, against those who insert these
advertisements. As I was not present at
Ascot this year, I thought I would try
what information these wise men could
impart to me about the likely results of
the races which were to take place, so I
sent £7, 14s. to thirteen of these self-styled
infallible prophets. The result was they
sent me nineteen winners, and ninety-five
losers, and four of them only sent me one
winner to thirty-five losers. I am glad to

say I did not yield to the temptation of backing their tips, or I fear, instead of being with you to-day, I should be chargeable to you on the rates, and you would be helping to support me in the workhouse."

I am perfectly aware that if I wrote from now until the crack of doom—whenever that may be—I should not stop punting, for in the words of old Thomas Carlyle, "The world contains so many million people, mostly fools."

WASTED TIME.

IF all the time that is wasted in the course of a year were accumulated it would amount to something considerable. Everybody wastes some portion of his or her time, possibly on the Indian's principle, that they have "all the time there is" to go at, and that they may as well fool with some of it.

Some people waste time because they have nothing else to do. They are blessed by the possession of such means as make labour not a necessity. Their existence is a perpetual state of *dolce far niente* and they do not count time, but as a means of regulating their movements and showing them how the years roll by. So they waste it at their ease in a pleasantly indolent way, and if they do no good with their time they do no harm. They are the butterflies of life, who, when the summer of England has ended its spasmodically miserable career, fly to other climes to waste the remainder of the year amid the flowers. Even the school-boy habitually wastes his time and spends as much of the day as he can looking at the lagging clock, and mentally wishing old Time would hurry up and arrive at the hour when lessons and tyrannical masters shall cease from troubling and the pupil be at rest.

What is the result? Arrived at manhood he finds he is behind his fellows in the race of life, and lives perpetually regretting that he wasted his time at school. Let him labour as he will he cannot recover the lost ground, and there will ever and anon crop up some unpleasant reminder of his wasted time. Terrible sinners in the matter of wasted time are the young men whose ages vary from eighteen to twenty-four. They do no more at business than bare necessity compels, and their evenings are wasted in aimless frivolity, if in nothing worse. They smoke heavily and, alas! too often, they drink heavily too. They spend their evenings in music-halls or public-houses.

Many of them indulge in that dangerous and far from remunerative amusement, small betting. They spend their meal hours in the company of betting men and loafers, and fondly imagine that they are becoming acquainted with the ways of the turf. Fatal delusion! They are only wasting their time and losing their money.

Any idea of utilising their spare time for the purposes of self-improvement never seems to strike these would-be mashers, the result being that their rise in the world of commerce is frequently a slow one, the prizes being taken by those of their fellows who have not wasted their time.

Believe me, wasted time is but a poor amusement at the best. Why, people who habitually waste their time do not even know how to enjoy legitimately-earned rest. There is nothing more enjoyable in life than the brief respite of the busy man, who, feeling he has not wasted his time during the remainder of the year, lays himself out to enjoy to the full a well-earned holiday.

There are men whose wasted time is tinged with sadness. Men who toil and labour through long years of suffering to attain a given end, and all to no purpose. Poor inventors whose busy brains toil through the long nights when the work of the day is over, toil, invent, and scheme, only to find when the labour is over and the day of life is far spent that for lack of the wherewithal to carry on the work it must be given up, and the loving care and anxious thought of years must, upon the eve of completion, be abandoned.

Verily this is the irony of Fate; and such wasted time merits the sympathy of those who think. Another inventor who does not merit sympathy, but who wastes time on his hobby, is the man who will invent things no one is ever likely to require. A peculiarity about the results of his wasted time is that his patents invariably fail to act when put into use, and he lives in a continual state of scheming improvements for inventions which are condemned as impracticable. All to no purpose ; he lacks the constructive ability and the grit necessary to work out details with care and accuracy, and the result once more is wasted time.

An awful example of wasted time comes from the arena where resides the terrible bugbear of Society — the amateur poet. Now he *can* waste time, though it would take half-a-dozen men of average talent to convince him of the fact. You cannot stem the flow of his so-called poetic eloquence. He has even survived the English springs of the past few years, and while his fellows have been railing at the clerk of the weather and swearing the climate was going to the dogs, he has trotted out his verse with stolid regularity and pointed out to the grumblers that they had their eyes shut; and has shown them beauties which they in their benighted state had failed to find. A wonderful man is the spring poet.

But he wastes his time; for his poems either repose at the bottom of the editorial waste-paper basket or are returned with the editor's compliments — "declined with thanks."

And so the world wags, and time is wasted in many ways by many people who, if they but took the trouble to utilise the time they waste, might put it to profitable use, both for themselves and their fellows.

MARRIED LIFE.

THERE is an old proverb which says, that "married life is either Hell or Heaven," and experience has proved that it is a tolerably fair estimate of the ordinary results of matrimony.

Marriage, as a rule, is the result of a chapter of circumstantial accidents, that is when it is not deliberately planned for the purpose of connecting families and property, or with the object of alleviating the impecuniosity of the aristocracy by means of the wealth of the democracy.

If a poll could be honestly taken of the majority of middle-class benedicts, it would, I doubt not, be found that a very large percentage of them regretted their marriages, and would, were it not for the opinion of their world, have sought freedom in divorce ere they had been wedded a couple of years.

If all men and women could find their ideals and marry them, then matrimony would be the perfection of Utopia, but as few ever do so, it remains one of the lotteries of life—a lottery which, in the old sweet way, contains more blanks than prizes. As a matter of fact, the process of drifting is responsible for a great many marriages, and many a man has married a girl because he found he had drifted into a position he never dreamed of, but which he could not very well get out of without the risk of an action-at-law. This kind of marriage as often turns out what the world calls a satisfactory one as otherwise. Without being actually in love the contracting parties have a certain feeling of respect and affection for each other, and even if, in their saner moments, they find they have made a mistake, they take the bull by the horns and mutually decide to

make the best of a bad job. Nothing of a
serious character ensues in the family
mansion, and they both settle down to a
humdrum life of monotonous domesticity
with placid resignation, finding such solace
for their wasted existence as their children
and their home afford. They are happy in
an aimless sort of way, and go on vegetating until they cross the bar with the
satisfaction in their hearts that they have
done their duty to their children and not
done any material wrong to their fellow-
creatures.

Not so the woman who really loves. To
her, marriage with the man she worships
—and these women do worship—is Elysium,
the Alpha and Omega of life. She is the
personification of the line, "love is of man's
life a part; 'tis woman's whole existence."
To her there is no such thing as respect in
wedded life; she gives herself body and
soul to her husband, and so long as her
faith in him be not shattered she is his

slave, ready to do his bidding, and to share his adversity with the same grace that she shares his prosperity.

But once she discovers that he is in any way playing her false she becomes a changed woman. Love turns to contempt, and if she does not take the course of criminality, she lapses into a state of coldness that is not calculated to create a feeling of affection in the household. From this state she in another way drifts also, but is drifting from her home and her husband, and she seeks elsewhere for the balm of love she cannot obtain at home.

The end is easily foretold. She comes across another man, and, in the feigned adoration he supplies, finds solace for a wounded pride and a shattered faith. No need to follow the play to the fall of the curtain. It has been too often paraded before an edified public through the medium of the Divorce Court.

And thus it is and thus it will be until

humanity be transformed and the passions of men and women altered. Married life is a game of chance, and it only requires the hand of Fate to hold an unseen card in the rubber of life to upset the best-laid schemes of men and women.

The moral is obvious. If you marry, do so prepared to make the best you can of the results, and if you find the right woman, guard her as you would a jewel of the greatest value. Do not expect wives or husbands to be immaculate, and never make mountains out of mole-hills. Never meet trouble half-way, and always remember that to err is human, to forgive divine.

MODERN schemes for the education of the masses have taken various forms, and have been more or less appreciated by the great unwashed. It has long been considered that a great factor in the artistic and intellectual education of the middle classes is the picture gallery. It is argued by those specially interested in the matter that an acquaintance with pictures and other works of art must of necessity have a refining influence on the minds of the people. With this idea in view, picture galleries have been erected and filled with pictures from the brushes of artists ancient and modern. Æstheticism has been rampant of late years, and the disciples of floral worship and flopping attitudes have laboured vigorously to imbue the minds of the public with their peculiar cult.

We have been told the bright colours—which Mr Ruskin considers the delight of healthy humanity—are *outré*, and that the true artistic sense only deals in half tones. Dingy greens and sickly yellows have been held forth as typical of æsthetic colour, and peacocks' feathers have been held in high esteem. It has further been put forth that it was the correct thing to languish over lilies and to pose over poppies—in " stained - glass attitudes " of the most uncomfortable kind.

All this has been done by a body of enthusiasts whose efforts were intended to create a purer taste in the minds of the masses. Some of the results of their efforts are to be seen in our picture galleries to-day, where æsthetic maidens of lank proportions are portrayed on canvas with appearances which suggest phthisis and the attendance of the family doctor. The painting disciples of the cult are given over body and soul to repose, and they depict pallid young men and maidens in a perpetual state of yearning—principally, it seems to me, for the unattainable. This idea I have gleaned from the various scraps of poetry usually appended to the titles of æsthetic pictures in exhibition catalogues. Æsthetic poets all yearn. It seems to do them good. I have even known an æsthetic poet try to transfer the yearning of his poems to canvas. The result was astounding. Yet, in spite of the efforts of the æsthetic there is, judging from the usual contents of our galleries, much work left for them to accomplish ere their mission can be said to be completed. They have still to grapple with the demon of mediocrity which reigns in every collection of pictures outside the National Gallery, and is particularly rampant in provincial exhibitions.

Professor Herkomer once said, " Beware

of old masters," and he might with equal
force have added " and budding painters,"
for their efforts do much to weaken the
educating effect of work of real merit,
They are the artistic old men of the sea,
and hang on to the edge of the world of
art, and gain a false reputation from the
mere fact of having their pictures placed
side by side with the work of abler men.

A lengthy experience of picture galleries
and exhibitions has gradually brought the
conviction to my mind that there are fewer
real artists in our island than one would
be led to suppose from the amount of art
talk and literature periodically placed before
the public. For one artist with invention,
colour, sense, and mastery of technique,
there are hundreds who have none of these
qualities, but who are merely the producers
of better-class " pot-boilers "—mere imitators
of the genuine artist.

A type of picture which is specially
annoying and is to be met with in all

galleries, is the one which figures in the
catalogue as "The Portrait of a Lady."
The lady's name is never given, and much
anxiety of mind is thus caused to spectators
as to the identity of the lady in question.
How are they to tell whether the portrait
be good or bad? For anything they
know the lady may be entirely different
to the picture, and therefore it is simply
a waste of time to express an opinion as
to the accuracy of the production. These
anonymous portraits invariably show that
the ladies who are thus painted have a
special weakness for evening dress, and are
in the habit of displaying as much of the
human form divine as the laws of society
and decency permit. Then, there are the
artists who will paint small children in
large bonnets which seem to have be-
longed to their grandmothers. The children
always appear to be intensely uncomfortable, and give one the impression that
they have been undergoing the operation

of sitting for their photographs. In the catalogue they appear as "Cherry Ripe," "Little Mrs Gamp," "Little Miss Muffit," and other equally inappropriate names. Occasionally they are depicted as impersonating their elders, and then they are re-named and appear in the catalogues under such titles as "I'm Grandmamma" or "The Little Mother." But they are always the same children with the same doll-like expression of irritating sweetness. One never, by any chance, sees them out of a picture gallery, and it must be intensely exasperating to the father of a family to know that his own offspring fall so far short of the child-standard set up by the modern painters. These children are generally painted full-face, for if by any chance the artist painted them in profile, their bonnets would entirely preclude the possibility of their faces being seen.

Anyone taking up a catalogue of a

picture exhibition at random, might with reason conclude that the study of phrenology was largely practised by modern painters, for no exhibition is complete without it has several specimens of the type of picture known as "A Study of a Head." This specimen of art is perhaps one degree less interesting than "The Portrait of a Lady," for you are not only at the same disadvantage in reference to whose head has been studied, but there is an entire absence of information as to the result of the study. Really, painters should be more considerate. Another annoying style of picture comes from the artists who paint marine subjects. It generally consists of a tremendous quantity of sea and sky and one or two small boats, so diminutive as to be almost indistinguishable. This style of picture usually figures in the catalogue as "Fishing Boats off Scarborough," "An Approaching Storm," or "A Sea Piece, with Shipping." The painters of this style of picture are remarkable for the large amount of canvas they cover, and the small amount of detail they put on to its surface. Their subjects are so manipulated that almost any title having reference to things marine would fit them. This is convenient and must save them an immensity of thought in the matter of selection. " Homely pathetic" subjects are immensely popular with the painters of better-class "potboilers," and in all galleries are to be found pictures of sorrowing wives and weeping children, whose respective and respected relatives have gone to the bourne from whence no traveller returns. By way of equalising this phase of art you may occasionally find a picture dealing with the return of a warrior from the wars or a prodigal to the paths of rectitude. Few of the "homely pathetic" pictures touch a real chord of sympathy, and are as a rule more provocative of laughter than tears.

This is especially noticeable when a domestic subject is taken in hand by a front-rank artist, for the very delicacy with which he handles his subject shows up the coarseness and crudeness of the exponents of mediocrity who rely solely on the strength of their subjects (frequently worn threadbare) for their success with the crowd.

Now, it seems to me that our picture galleries are too large, the result being that mediocrity flourishes where perfection alone should reign. To be the means of educating the masses, picture galleries should contain work from the best painters only, and the producers of mediocre pictures should be entirely barred. There is seldom, if ever, any beauty in second-rate pictures, and if nothing but the best examples of English and foreign art were admitted to our galleries, the taste of the public would be trained in the right direction and their artistic instincts would gradually become horoughly developed. Promoters of art exhibitions will, I am fully aware, argue that it would be most difficult to obtain such a collection as I advocate, but that does not alter the facts. So long as "potboilers" are admitted wholesale to exhibitions, so long will there be sneering from the cultivated and want of appreciation from the crowd. Beauty, whether in colour or form, appeals to all; but when it is dwarfed by surroundings of ugliness and mediocrity, it loses a large percentage of its power of attraction.

FADS AND FADDISTS.

THE old Yorkshireman who is reputed to have said, "There's nowt so queer as folks," might with perfect veracity have added that there was an equal amount of peculiarity about the fads of the said "folks." Fads are extraordinary things, and one never knows how they spring into existence. They may be non-existent one day and in full bloom the next. They grow with all the rapidity of the mushroom and depart with snail-like slowness. They are like their possessors, of all sorts and conditions, and do not confine themselves to any particular sphere of life. Young men and maidens, old men and children are all liable to them, and old ladies who have not had the fortune or misfortune to enter the state of matrimony often get most of the sweetness of their lives out of them.

Not only individuals but organisations are subject to the effects of fads, and it is to a peculiar fad—more or less authenticated—of the late Earl of Beaconsfield, that we owe the existence of Primrose Day and Primrose Leagues. Politicians and Puritans, Saints and Sinners alike are all victims to fads. In fact, "the world is a *melée* of special constables, each bent upon getting his own fad enforced at the point of the truncheon." Had there never been any fads there would have been no mashers, and high collars and their accompanying discomforts would not have existed. Fads are responsible for more things in this world than a casual observer would be tempted to imagine. Men take things up as fads, and by sticking to them long enough in many cases produce results undreamed of at the time the fad took possession of them. Take the case of a man with a taste for mechanics. He potters about in his miniature workshop experimenting at his leisure. It is his fad. One day he discovers that some improvement might be made in the tools he is using, and he sets to work to find out how. The result is a patent that not only enriches the inventor, but proves of practical use to a portion of the world at large. Simply the result of a fad.

But there are fads which do not carry with them the redeeming feature of usefulness, and their possessors are, not unfrequently, a nuisance to their friends and acquaintances. For instance, there is the ventilating faddist, a being who has a theory for remedying all errors of atmosphere and temperature. Once let him get a foothold in your homestead and you are doomed. He will never leave you, but your peace of mind will. He will tell you the exact amount of cold air necessary for the preservation of good health, and if your

rooms be pleasantly warm and comfortable
he will, even on the coldest day, talk
scientifically about vitiated atmosphere until
you feel it is your bounden duty to open
all the windows in spite of the fact that
you are subject to rheumatism and neuralgia.
He is a walking catalogue of patent venti-
lators, and the vigour of his recommenda-
tions is suggestive of a commission on
results. Another faddist is the man with
a mania for old china, which he accumulates
to the full extent his means will allow.
This faddist is very often a living proof
of the veracity of the adage that a little
knowledge is a dangerous thing. He will
buy almost anything, provided it be a pot,
and has an appearance of age. Therefore,
on the principle that people with brains
and no money are made for the benefit
of people with money and no brains, certain
dealers in modern - ancient pottery provide
for his delectation a choice selection of
pots of more or less value—principally the

latter—which they palm off for the real
articles at prices commensurate with their
value as genuine relics of departed ages.
In spite of this, he is perfectly happy in
the enjoyment of his fad ; and unless some
unkind friend shatters his happiness by
proving his collection more or less worthless, he will end his days in the belief
that he is an authority on Ceramic art, and
that his collection is of the utmost value.
He is not the only faddist who lives in a
dreamland of his own. The peculiarity of
his pots is their intense ugliness. This is
supposed to add to their value.

Then there is the man who has a peculiar
fad in reference to medicine and the pro-
viders thereof. His pet aversion is a
medical man, and he will insist upon doc-
toring himself. He has a large collection of
medical dictionaries and cyclopædias, and
keeps a miscellaneous assortment of drugs
and patent medicines on the premises. If
by any accident you tell him you are not

feeling quite up to the mark, he at once pre-
scribes for you, and suggests an alternative
list of medicines, patent and otherwise.

As an ally to the ventilating faddist he
would be invaluable—from a doctor's point
of view. He says it saves doctor's bills, but
it is a peculiar thing that all his knowledge is of no avail when he is taken
seriously ill. On the contrary, he is invariably told by the despised doctor he is
compelled to call in that he has been doing his level best to ruin his constitution
generally and has materially lessened his
chances of recovery in the case immediately in question. This faddist is one
whom experience cannot teach, for no
sooner does he recover (under the treat-
ment of his pet aversion) than he is as
ready as ever to fly to his old fads when
he feels unwell. Foolish faddist! If he
but knew it, he is spending more money on
worthless nostrums than would pay for advice
and medicine from a reliable practitioner.

I once knew a man who had a fad as to the peculiar style of cloth he used for his trousers. He always wore a peculiar large check pattern, and ordered his breeches by the dozen pairs. Winter or summer he never changed his check (no imputation as to his commercial stability intended). If he be living still, he is certain to be wearing the same check trousers as of yore. The principal objection to this peculiar fad was that it gave people the impression that its owner never got a new pair of trousers. And such a notion is hardly one a man would care for his friends to entertain. Yet I verily believe the man would have sooner given up a friend or two than have given up his beloved check. You couldn't check his fad. There are certainly some advantages attached to a large check. It is not only distinctive, but it can, on occasion, be used with advantage as a substitute for a draught-board.

A faddist who is a nuisance to many people is the man or woman who desires to possess what an eminent journalist once called "an indiscriminate collection of other people's signatures." In a word I mean the autograph-hunter. He, it is generally a man, usually goes very mad on his fad, but there is monetary method in his madness. He has no sense of delicacy, and gathers in his, or other people's, signatures with an eye to the main chance, for autographs have a saleable value. He will worry the life out of a celebrity with a persistence worthy of a better cause, and having at last obtained his prize will show it in triumph to his friends, with an intimation that he saw the same celebrity's autograph advertised for sale in a paper for a certain sum of money. He worries his victims in all sorts of ways, and is for ever trying to invent new methods for obtaining signatures from people who, like the late Charles Reade, think autograph collectors an emphatic nuisance.

And the old maid's fads, what are they?

"Silly," says the world. But are they in reality so? I think not. Are they not rather a cloak behind which lie hidden the sweetest memories of a happy girlhood; memories of a time when the flowers and blossoms of spring seemed laden with love, and the world but a garden where grew the flowers of hope and contentment. Believe me, there is much true sentiment and reverence pent up beneath the womanish fads the world sneers at, if only one had the key to the mystery. There is seldom any harm in the fads indulged in by the old ladies of the world, be they maids or widows. In both cases the peculiarities are invariably the outcome of departed days, and the sleek tabby, who is tended and cared for with a seeming extravagance by its maiden owner, knows it will never have a kinder mistress. The widow's fads usually take the form of idolising relics, and who shall grudge her the right to shed her heart-felt tears over a picture or a lock of hair?

To her they are not the inanimate things they are to us, they speak full eloquently of the past and bring to mind with vivid reality many pleasures long since passed away. Life is sad enough to those whose idols exist only in the mind, without the scoffers making fun of their little eccentricities. Therefore, do not sneer at the little fads which emanate from the corner of a woman's heart, where loving memories are stowed away and where the sunlight of departed hours still shines at intervals when the world is sleeping and she is alone with her thoughts.

THE WEATHER.

THERE is something terribly aggravating about weather in general, and the weather of this country in particular. It is so unreliable. There is no placing the slightest confidence in it, and the way it ignores the barometers and the prophets is simply appalling. It seems to have lost all sense of the fitness of things of · late years.

In the good old days of which we hear so much, we are told "the weather was worth calling weather." In those much vaunted days they had—so say the chroniclers—regular seasons, and spring, summer, autumn and winter, could be relied upon to turn up with the atmospheric surroundings expected in connection with them.

We have no such things now-a-days, and snow-storms in July are as likely to be chronicled as the fact that there is not the slightest use for skates from December to March. The whole system is disarranged. And the erratic movements of the weather seem to have been more pronounced since the Americans began to anticipate it by their prior-to-date forecasts. When you come to look at it, the thing is hardly surprising, and the perverse way in which the weather upsets the tables of the prophets may he put down as its practical and peculiar method of telling interfering weather prophets to mind their own business, and not interfere with things they do not understand. I say this may be the case, but, whatever be the cause, there is a wide difference between the prophets and the weather they predict. For the sake of suffering humanity they really ought to

try and conciliate the elements. The uncertainty of the elements is likely to result
in an unlooked-for calamity, for it will, if
it goes on, put to rout a stock theme of
conversation. For years the weather has
been the great subject for opening or helping on a conversation, and the salutation,
"Good morning, glorious morning, isn't it?"
has frequently led to many an interesting
chat. Then how entertaining and interesting the discussions as to the probable
weather the day would bring forth. The
man who foretold rain felt that if his
friend did not provide for the coming
downpour he had not any confidence in his,
the prophet's, acumen. And if it did rain,
how self-satisfied he felt. Now, this kind
of conversation is apt to be dangerous, for
so erratic have the elements become that
at the very moment you are stating it is a
fine day, it is as likely as not that the
rain will come down in torrents, and the
people to whom you have expressed your

opinion will go away with the impression that you are not an observant person, which is, to say the least of it, annoying. A curious phase of remarks relating to the weather is that they are mostly bare statements of fact which must be palpable to everyone they are made to. It has always seemed to me to be an inference that there is something wanting in a man's powers of perception to tell him in the midst of blue sky and bright sunshine that it is a fine day, or to inform him when the rain is spoiling his best suit and getting through his thin shoes that it is a wet one. Yet these absurd truisms are repeated by the hundred daily, whereas on any other subject than the weather people would as soon think of flying as of indulging in them.

I suppose the fact is that weather has become such an anomaly that people do not consider it worth treating rationally. And then look at the way it treats the spring poets, who must be imbued with a faith only equalled by that of a Salvation Army soldier in his General. Season after season they try to convince the world that spring is all they paint it—a lovely season where nature and the birds burst forth with equal success. But it won't do in the present state of affairs. There is nothing poetic about catarrh, and very little sentiment attached to influenza. But they both come round with the spring. If things go on as they are much longer, the calendar will have to be re-arranged, and the positions of the various seasons transposed. But even then there would be no certainty that the weather might not, just for spite, turn round altogether. It might be worth while to try the experiment on the off-chance.

There is a keen sense of annoyance experienced when one looks at some of the old pictures dealing with picnics and other pleasures of the summer. Picnics, in the pictures, are depicted as taking place in the midst of the most delightful weather and surroundings. The light gauzy frocks of the ladies flutter in the breeze, and the flannels of the gentlemen tell of the heat of a glorious afternoon. This is in the pictures. Now-a-days the whole thing is changed, and people go to picnics with a liberal supply of macintoshes and umbrellas, and have their pleasure largely spoiled by anticipations of a visit from Jupiter Pluvius. And yet we are living in the much-praised nineteenth century, with its phonographs, its electric light, and its scientific research. The Australian prelate who refused to pray for rain on the ground that the people did not give the rain a chance had, in all probability, other reasons for his non-compliance with his flock's request. He doubtless knew how unreliable the weather is, and he did not care to experiment where the prophets and the almanacks had failed. He was a wise man.

One thing that it is always safe to do when dealing with the weather is to grumble at it and sneer at the weather forecasts and their producers. Not only does this relieve you, but it coincides with the feelings of your friends who grumble with you in a sympathetic spirit.

If the weather prophets would get within reasonable distance of the weather they might be tolerated, but when they prophesy storms they don't come, and when their prognostications point to delightful weather it is certain to rain. And yet there are people who daily turn to the forecasts in their morning papers with a firm belief that they are going to be informed with accuracy as to the kind of weather that will be around during the day. Poor deluded mortals! They are the people whom experience does not teach. They store up old almanacks, and when, by accident, a prophecy comes off they show it to their friends, and tell of the wonders in

store for them in the way of weather pre-
dictions for the future. They are judici-
ously silent as to the failures of their
pet prophets. These people live in fond
anticipation that some of these days we
shall again be favoured with that much-
talked of season, "a good old-fashioned
Christmas."

As it is no use crying over spilt milk (it
only makes it more watery, as H. J. Byron
said), so it is but little use to shed tears
about the failure of the prophets and the
state of the weather. We can only growl
and bear it, and wait patiently until such
times as it sees fit to leave off fooling and
stick to its business with some semblance
of seriousness. It has got on the loose,
and, as is usual in such cases, it will have
to have its own time to come round in.

So in the meantime we can only study
the almanacks, barometers and forecasts, in
the hope that one of these days things
may get righted. At the same time let us

get what consolation we can from the lines of that truthful idyl which says,

> " Whether it's cold or whether it's hot
> We've got to weather it, whether or not."

PEOPLE WHO WANT TO KNOW.

WITHOUT the pale of that educational arena where the thirst for information is fostered by Act of Parliament, and where children and their elders are crammed with varied knowledge until they can pass examinations at the rate of 98 and 99 per cent., there exists a class of people who, with no regard to educational advancement, are always wanting to know something. If you volunteer an ordinary piece of information, or tell them the state of affairs in relation to certain events, they do not rest satisfied with the bare statement supplied, but at once ask why such a state of affairs exists? They want to know the cause for each effect of life, and more especially so if it be domestic. Whether they thoroughly attend to their own business may be ques-

tioned; but that they take a deep and
continual interest in other people's admits
of no possible doubt whatever. You see
they want to know, and if some of the
means whereby they gain their ends are
open to criticism, they do not consider
that; and if asked why they thus endeavour to lay bare the skeletons in the
domestic cupboards of other people, they
invariably give as their illogical reason
that they want to know. They ferret out
a cause for the actions of their neighbours,
they wonder why the Government does
not alter its plans in accordance with their
own ideas, and they see nothing objectionable in their wanting to know the income
and expenditure of their friends and acquaintances. In fact, they ask so many
questions and want to know so much that
there always seems to be considerable
danger of their developing into peregrinat-
ing notes of interrogation. Heavy sinners
in this respect are the daughters of Eve.

It seems to be part of their constitution to annex, during their lives, an unique collection of more or less accurate information about things in general, and their friends in particular. If these ladies were not so fond of " wanting to know," the tongue of scandal would be silenced, and the pleasures of afternoon tea would depart.

From the cradle to the grave the thirst for indiscriminate information is gradually developed; and children are, with less evil results than their elders, great delinquents in the direction of wanting to know. For instance, when Master Johnny, *ætat* four, is told that he has become the possessor of a new sister, he at once begins to ask questions, and immediately wants to know where his relative came from? On his nurse, with the absence of veracity usual on such occasions, informing him that the latest addition to the household was found "under the gooseberry bush," he evinces a desire to know which particular bush it

was, and at the same time suggests a
voyage of discovery with a view to possible
contingencies in the direction of a further
supply of relatives. Should the fairy-tale
be that the doctor brought the new arrival
with him in his pocket, Master Johnny
shows that he has doubts as to the holding
capacity of the said pocket, and straightway proposes to interview the doctor on
the subject. He wants to know. Another
species of want - to - know people are the
individuals who write to newspapers and
weekly journals for information, and who
expect to be supplied with it immediately
—if not sooner.

They expect editors of papers, and especially such papers as are labelled "domestic," to be walking catalogues of facts and
fashions, periods and passions; and they
worry them week after week with queries
on every conceivable subject, which they
fondly imagine will be answered in their particular paper the same week they send them.

I have lately perused much literature, if it can so be called, of the "Answers to Correspondents" order, and I cannot but think that the ordinary (and now and then extraordinary) readers who want to know must have a high and reliable opinion of the modern editor. Their faith is a thing to dream about. You cannot shake it. They pour their secret troubles into the editorial ear, as though the literary ruler were a priest and his office and waste-paper basket but details of the confessional. In this connection readers of the better-class sensational weeklies of the *Family Herald* type are perhaps the worst sinners. They fancy the editor of their pet paper ought to be able to advise them on any domestic difficulty they may meet with, and in the matter of love, courtship and marriage, they would sooner take his opinion than that of a dream-book or a gipsy. He ought to feel flattered, but I am much afraid he will not see the faith in his powers in that way.

He hasn't time to go into the niceties of the situation — it takes him all his time to answer the questions sent him each week. Let us glance at one or two queries sent by ladies who are incapable of managing their love - affairs and their young men. Here is a damsel who has, apparently, not yet learned the art of hooking her fish. She writes to a popular weekly, and this is the state of affairs she desires the editor to straighten up :—" In Suspense " has for five years been receiving the attentions of a gentleman, but with hardly any understanding whatever. Now he avoids her. What is she to do ? Should she write to him for an explanation ? Now, as the editor could not possibly know either the young man or " In Suspense," he could — as he did — only generalise on the state of affairs with the result that his reply left the lady exactly where she was. If correspondents only knew it, the domestic affairs of their editorial idol keep him as fully occupied as it is desirous in the interests of his non-corresponding readers he should be. Married men usually object to being bothered with other people's experiences of the unevenness of the path of true (more or less) love. You see they have travelled the road themselves. Still, in spite of good advice and gently administered sarcasm, the correspondent still flourishes and tells his or her tales of blighted affection or broken vows with an objectionable regularity. I am beginning to think that these ill-used lovers and perplexed maidens rather glory in their crosses. It gives them an opportunity of writing to an editor; and I am firmly convinced that they gloat over the replies in the seclusion of their bedrooms and begin to have a glimmering and fatal suspicion that they may one day become authors and write for the papers. And all the outcome of wanting to know.

Another of the want-to-know order to be

avoided is the man who writes queries on etiquette. He is a social terror. Judging from the number of questions this individual asks, one might conclude that he ought not to be allowed out without a guide. If he be as ignorant of the rules of Society as his questions suggest, he might in all fairness be expected to take his soup with a fork and peas with his fingers. If his ignorance be not assumed he may be pardoned for wanting to know.

Then there is the old lady, with money, who wants to know how to make a will, and who never seems struck with the idea that she might consult a solicitor, who would not only relieve her anxiety in the present but prevent litigation in the future. Possibly the old lady has no belief in the lights of the law, and prefers to dispose of her goods and chattels without the aid of a solicitor. Well, experience has taught ere this, that men of law are not the pleasantest things to have about the house. They, too, frequently want to know.

Correspondents who ask the same questions are numerous, and the phrase "upwards of a hundred" seems to trouble the minds of not a few of them, for they ask the meaning of it unceasingly. Heights of mountains, depths of rivers, the age of actresses, and the value of shares are all things that people want to know through the medium of the papers they patronise. And if they don't get replies they write spiteful letters to the editor. You see they know that editors live out of the public, and they do not wish them to forget the fact.

And thus the world goes round and people all want to know. From the dazzling halls of light to the humble cottage there is a great and yearning desire to know about things and people, and Lady Geraldine de Montmorency is as eager to know the particulars of her dearest friend's *faux pas* as Mrs Mooney, the charwoman, is to hear the thrilling details of the latest disagreement between her friends and her neighbours, Mr and Mrs O'Flannigan. They are both actuated by the same desire, and curiosity is the mainspring which sets them on; and though mischief may result from their desire they do not generally act from motives of spite. They do it simply and solely because they want to know.

PANTOMIMES.

PANTOMIME, in its truest sense, has ceased to exist, and in this nineteenth century of culture and learning the public is treated to a mixture of music-hall fooling and harlequinade horseplay; a display of vulgarity and mediocrity which our fathers would have hissed off the stage had any theatrical manager had the audacity to present it to them. Yet season after season these inane—one might almost say insane—productions are to be seen in the best theatres, and thousands of pounds are spent in dressing and backing up pantomimes which are like unto pantomime proper as chalk is like unto cheese. Originally pantomimes were, as their name denotes, performances done in dumb show, and they are, on the authority of Geneste, said to have been introduced into England about the year 1723.

Colley Cibber tells of a pantomime piece founded on the story of "Mars and Venus," wherein the passions were so happily expressed, and the whole story so intelligibly told by a mute narration of gesture only, that even thinking spectators allowed it both a pleasing and rational entertainment. Now if it were possible so many years ago, when things theatrical were in their infancy, to tell in dumb show an intelligent story, how is it that to-day we are, in spite of our knowledge and experience, compelled to put up with pantomime wherein, nine times out of ten, the ordinary nursery tales beloved of the children are so badly handled by writers of pantomime books that they are as unintelligible as the dumb shows of the past were intelligible and entertaining. I was told, not long ago, by a stage manager of many years' experience,

that the book was almost of less importance than any other part of the machinery
of pantomime, and that the success or
failure of a modern pantomime depended
but to a small extent upon its author.

On this point I join issue with the
stage-manager, for if the *framework or construction* of a pantomime book be faulty,
I am certain, from experience, that the production will invariably run the risk of
failure. An author's lines, I admit, do not,
at this day, count for much.

And why?

For the very good and simple reason
that many of the people engaged are
unable to speak them. This tendency to
disregard the author is of recent growth,
and may, I think, be said to date from
the time when music-hall performers began
to usurp the places of legitimate actors and
actresses in pantomime.

Modern pantomime books are *made*, not
written, and it is this very introduction of

uneducated "speciality" people which is responsible for the downfall of interesting, sensible, and pleasing pantomimes.

I can remember the day when a pantomime writer took some pains with his book, filled it with smart lines, good puns, and topical and local hits.

In a book done for a theatre with a high reputation for pantomime, which I read the other day, I found all these essentials to success conspicuous by their absence.

In the days departed the actors and actresses paid full attention to the author, and made his points and lines tell with the audience. Now-a-days such a state of affairs is rare indeed. At a well-known provincial theatre recently a big star from the music halls was engaged to play a principal part in the Christmas show. On turning up at the first rehearsal he went to the stage-manager, and showing him his part said,—

"What's this for?"

"That's your part; you've got to learn it," replied the official.

"Learn this," said the astonished star; "why, it takes me twelve months to learn a song."

And the truth of his confession was fully demonstrated, for he never learned the part, and stuck to the text that he was "engaged to do his business," which consisted of singing so-called comic songs which were devoid of all the elements of humour.

It is performers of this order, and their name is legion, who kill all attempts on the part of the author, and who mar by their vulgarity and ignorance the best attempts at genuine pantomime.

As they are the bugbear of the author who has to write parts for them, so are they the bugbear of the manager, who, having engaged them at extravagant salaries, is bound to utilise such ability as they possess to the best advantage, and gener-

ally to the disadvantage of more talented
people, who, if they had the opportunity,
would do much to keep pantomime free from
the blots which are yearly to be seen in
it, even at the best theatres.

Even the songs introduced into modern
pantomime are, for the most part, entirely
and totally irrelevant to the subject on
which the book is based.

Yet they are put in year after year, and
people who would turn their eyes up in
pious horror if anyone suggested their visit-
ing a music hall listen, night after night,
to the very songs which have, during the
year, become the favourites of the music-
hall patrons. Why respectable and educated
people should be compelled to listen to a
song which tells of the adventures of a gay
young spark of not too moral habits, and
has for its catch-phrase the charming words,
"Hi Tiddley Hi, Ti Ti Ti," is one of the
things which, as Lord Dundreary put it,
"no fellah can understand." Yet songs of

this type are to be found in all the pantomimes throughout the country, and people
are paid big salaries for singing them.

The result is that the story suffers from
the fact that frequent opportunities have
to be given for the introduction of such
songs, and changes have to be made for the
benefit of people whose "business" must
go in somewhere and who can, in the
majority of cases, do nothing but the
special items they have hawked about
music-halls and pantomimes for years.

All of which points to, and strengthens,
my contention that the construction of a
pantomime is of more importance than many
people professionally interested are apt to
think.

Let the pantomime author lay down
clearly the framework of his story, indi-
cating where special items can be introduced without breaking the thread of his
tale, and modern pantomime would at least
be intelligible and rational, while there

would be no interference with the story
for the benefit of the *genus* music-hall
performer.

Until this be done, and done properly,
pantomime will continue to be an *ollo podrida* of absurdity with neither head, tail,
nor middle.

Another danger of modern pantomime is
the damage it does to the reputation of
artists of high standing in the world
dramatic. Unless the parts they are provided with have a strong connection with
the story, which is seldom the case, they
are certain to be overshadowed by the
rough horseplay of the music-hall people
in the cast, whose only idea is to get
laughs, no matter how they get them.
Many a clever legitimate comedian, engaged
at a high salary, has failed in pantomime
owing to a bad part and a preponderance
of "speciality" turns.

Bad parts are always the *bête noir*
of the actor, but in the legitimate drama

he is not hampered by horse-collar comedians
as he invariably is in modern pantomime.
Thus a bad or ill-fitting part in pantomime
is but the prelude to certain failure to
the artistic comedian, who is not able to
compete fairly with those inartistic nonde-
scripts to whom a part is of no consequence provided they get an opening in a
big scene for their special business. They
are the little old men of the sea of
pantomime, and by their tenacity and
cheek do more with their limited stock-
in-trade than the actor or actress can do
after years of experience and training, for
he or she is baulked and blocked at every
turn and corner by the inartistic buffoonery
of the mechanical and misnamed music-hall
" comedian."

SYMPATHY.

THERE is no feeling in the whole range of the human passions calculated to do so much good at so small a personal cost as sympathy. It appeals to rich and poor alike, and is as highly valued by a peer as by a peasant, and is equally at the command of both.

Sympathy is the balm that soothes the wounded feelings and helps to smooth the rough corners of life ; is far more potent than any medicine, and has this difference from that objectionable commodity that it is usually received with heartfelt joy and leaves no taint or taste behind it when it has done its work.

From the cradle to the grave sympathy plays an important part in the affairs of this fleeting life of ours, and many a child has had its budding ideas crushed out of it from the want of sympathy. The mother alone knows thoroughly the value of sympathy among children, and many a little one has been coaxed into the development of talents which might otherwise have been allowed to drift, and thus have been lost to the world in which they were in after years to play an important part. There is nothing more fatal to the enlargement of a child's ideas than constant snubbing, and if parents and teachers would use a little more sympathy than they frequently do, there would be many happier and brighter children in the world than there are at present. This fact is well known to the better class of teachers, who are quick to sympathise with their charges and are ever ready to foster and develop any peculiar phase of character or genius that may assert itself during the period children are under them.

What can be more tender than the sympathy of a woman to a sister in misfortune—the jilted lover or the sorrowing wife bereaved of her first-born or her husband? To a woman placed in such a position the sympathy of her sex is more precious than gold, and many a woman has gone out of her mind ere this, from the mere fact that she had no one to sympathise with her, no sister to whom she could open the flood-gates of her heart and with freely-flowing tears lay her tired head upon her breast and gain consolation and sympathy in her hour of need.

Apart from the phases already touched upon, sympathy enters largely into other scenes of life. To the artist, sympathy is equally as valuable as applause, and even the actor, who is usually supposed to live upon the latter, knows in his heart, if he be an artistic performer, that sympathy is of equal or greater importance than the plaudits of a well-pleased audience.

Even the statesman strives to earn the sympathy of nations, and if he fails to gain the sympathy of his constituents at election times, his chances of success are certain to be small.

Sympathy is a great factor in the ruling of the world, and if it be wisely and generously used may be calculated to do a vast amount of good, while, if withheld, it may frequently cause desolation and despair to enter the homes of the rich and poor alike.

DREAMS.

"DREAMS," says the poet, "are but the phantasy of an idle brain," and there is no doubt that the dreams of the ordinary day-dreamer are the result of his having no special object to occupy his mind. Yet, even in the busy hive of commerce you frequently find dreamers, men who, while deeply engaged in the exercise of their calling, still dream in the respites from their duties, and hope in the days to come to find their dream-hopes realised. But they seldom live to see the consummation of their desires. Why? Generally because their dreams are of the impossible. The possession of wealth without work, or of the Utopia, where everyone is happy, and where the worries and anxieties of life have no existence.

Then, on the other hand, there are the men whose dreams of avarice—never to be realised—only help to bring a sordid bitterness into their lives and to make the careers of those with whom they are connected sunless and unhappy. The contented man seldom dreams, at least not in this direction, and he fares far better than the greed-loving grinder of men who knows no sympathy, and who looks upon his *employés* as mere machines to be used for the purpose of aiding him in his attempts to realise his godless and hell-chained ambitions. This man's dreams are the ghosts of his days and nights, and he goes to rest—if such a man can rest—with his head full of speculative schemes, and wakes up to go forth into the world to achieve, if possible, at any cost his avaricious purpose. Poor fool! What will it avail him in the end even should he succeed? Nothing, for to the fell sergeant the millionaire is not more than his maid-servant, or the king one whit the greater than the peasant. His dreams, unfulfilled, caused him misery of mind, and when by chance they become tangible realities they usually result, after his death, in family feuds caused by the contents of his will and the planting of thorns in the bosoms of those who hoped to reap the benefit of the dreamer's toiling and misery.

Thus end his dreams, and he leaves the world more miserable than he found it, unwept and unloved.

Everybody dreams. Even the little ones. The gay little maiden just budding in the spring-time of life, has her day-dreams. Lovely visions of the time when she will go out into the gay world and see its full-blown flowers and inhale to the full their fragrance. As she grows older her dreams increase, and the horizon of her visions becomes a wider, if not a

happier one. She learns in time that the
flowers are not all fragrant with the per-
fume of love and happiness, but that the
rose and lily may grow side by side with
blossoms less fragrant and less beautiful.
Poor child, 'tis a pity her day-dreams are
not with her for ever, that the joy they
bring to her in the hours of her silent
meditation has to be rudely shattered by
the stern realities of a common-place existence, where the dreams of domesticity are
of a peace that hinges on the impossible,
and where a perpetual round of monotony
teaches her that dreaming is a thing to
avoid or to exist only of the memories of
the past, or the epitaphs of the "might-
have-been."

The schoolboy dreams of the day when
he will be a man and set the world on
fire with his prowess or his ingenuity. He
dreams of the proud period of life when
he will discard knickerbockers for trousers,
and "go to business like father."

There is a story told of a youthful aspirant for fame, whose dreams evidently took a practical turn, for on being asked by a casual acquaintance what he was going to be when he grew up, answered, "The same as father, sir." "And what is father?" queried the questioner. To which the lad replied solemnly, "Oh! he's a bishop, sir."

That boy knew something!

But there are some lads whose dreams are not of this order, and who in their little minds have dreaming tendencies in the direction of the future. The lad, who with no hint from others, thinks he would like to be an engineer or a soldier is but dreaming, and if parents and guardians were willing to help him in the direction he desires to go, instead of thinking for him they would frequently make a more than averagely useful citizen of him instead of condemning him to a life of commercial drudgery, which he loathes and which takes all the ambition out of him, and only adds one more soul to the great army of middle-class mediocrity.

Thus it is all the world over. Dreams and disappointment go hand-in-hand, and for one case of happy realisation there are thousands of waiting mortals whose dreams, first coming in the hey-day of life with the freshness of hope, gradually sink behind the clouds of despair and overshadow with their gloom and heartrendings their journey to the land where the dreamers cease from dreaming, and the weary are at rest.

SLEEP? AN ALLEGORY.

Last night I dreamed a dream. And lo, "I wakened in a strange, sad place, shadowed in gloom and dreamy mystery." A place where revelry held high domain, and wildest pleasure ruled the roost around. There lovely women and majestic men were lolling idly by a running stream whose waters murmured as they flowed along into a weird, unearthly song, the cadence of which seemed to form itself into this refrain :—

> Leisure and pleasure are joys for aye,
> Dance thro' the night and drink thro' the day ;
> Curse on the past and the future unknown
> Love and delight in the present we own.

The wine flowed freely, and luxurious love seemed monarch of the place. The women syrens kissed their yearning lords, whose lips were eager for their ruby touch.

And then methought I joined the throng and was surrounded by a bevy of golden-haired damsels whose arms stretched forward to entwine my neck. Lovely they were, yet in my inmost soul I feared and dreaded what their kiss might bring.

At last they left me—all but one; a sad-eyed maiden with a face so fair that mortal man had sold his soul to death and hell for but one hour of her love and life.

We strayed into a shaded grove apart from the laughing crowd, and there intently in her eyes I gazed and let the fetters of my heart lie loose. Once did her rose-lips touch my cheek and straight within me rose a wild desire to possess her, body and soul, for ever. Her face changed to that of my angel upon earth for one brief second, and fame, honour, and wealth were as nought compared to the ecstasy of her sweet salute.

Then did we speak of love. With chang-

ing features and with mocking laugh she
spoke of the God of Love. Her fair smiles
vanished, and her eyes were filled with
scorn and hate. " Love," she said, " is the
mockery of life, the lode-star of despair
and death. It is the one passion that
brings broken hearts to women and hate
to men. It is the forerunner of shattered
faith, and nameless graves, and seared
victims—whose name is legion and whose
end is sleep." " But," I answered, " I have
loved on earth, and even now hold sacred
in my heart the image of my better angel,
whose love and faith are to me as the
lighthouse to the sinking mariner." Then
did the syren's mocking laugh ring out
once more, filling the scent-laden grove
with its grating notes, and twining her
graceful arms around me once again, she
whispered : " Listen and be warned. You
think she loves you. Make the most of
your joy, for ere your lease of life be run
her heart may change, her faith and love

turn into contempt and hate. And in some moment when you hold her to your heart with joy, she may crush your hopes for ever, and leave you cursing on life's barren shore. All women have one victim in their lives. It is their due as recompense for the broken hearts of their sisters who believed and fell. Take care you are not hers."

With this she pressed her lips to mine once more and left me. I tried to follow her but could not move. Some unseen power held me back, until with a mighty effort I broke the baneful bonds of sleep and woke—to find the grey dawn rising without, the beads of perspiration standing on my throbbing forehead, and myself murmuring in tones of agony:

"Oh, God, there is no hell like sleep."

THE END.

London: Digby, Long & Co., Publishers,
18 Bouverie Street, Fleet Street, E.C.

DIGBY, LONG & CO.'S
NEW NOVELS, STORIES, Etc.

IN ONE VOLUME, Price 6s.

NEW NOVEL BY DR ARABELLA KENEALY.

The Honourable Mrs Spoor. By the Author of "Some Men are such Gentlemen," "Dr Janet of Harley Street," etc. Crown 8vo, cloth, 6s.

[*Just out.*

NEW NOVEL BY ANNIE THOMAS (Mrs PENDER CUDLIP).

False Pretences. By the Author of "Allerton Towers," "That Other Woman," "Kate Valliant," "A Girl's Folly," etc., etc. Crown 8vo, cloth, 6s.

[*Second Edition.*

The *WORLD* says:—"Miss Annie Thomas has rarely drawn a character so cleverly as that of the false and scheming Mrs Colraine."

NEW NOVEL BY DR ARABELLA KENEALY.

Some Men are such Gentlemen. By the Author of "Dr Janet of Harley Street," "Molly and Her Man-o'-War," etc. Crown 8vo, cloth, 6s. With a Frontispiece. [*Fifth Edition.*

The *ACADEMY* says:—"We take up a book by Miss Arabella Kenealy confidently expecting to be amused, and in her latest work we are not disappointed. The story is so brightly written that our interest is never allowed to flag. The heroine, Lois Clinton, is sweet and womanly. . . . The tale is told with spirit and vivacity, and shows no little skill in its descriptive passages."
The *PALL MALL GAZETTE* says:—"A book to be read breathlessly from beginning to end. It is decidedly original . . . its vivid interest. The picture of the girl is admirably drawn. The style is bright and easy."
TRUTH says:—"Its heroine is at once original and charming."

NEW NOVEL BY DORA RUSSELL.

The Other Bond. By the Author of "A Hidden Chain," "A Country Sweetheart," "The Drift of Fate," etc. Crown 8vo, cloth, 6s. [*Third Edition.*

The *ATHENÆUM* on Miss Russell's Works, says:—"Miss Russell writes easily and well, and she has the gift of making her characters describe themselves by their dialogue, which is bright and natural."

NEW NOVEL BY L. T. MEADE.

A Life for a Love. By the Author of "The Medicine Lady," "A Soldier of Fortune," "In an Iron Grip," etc., etc. Crown 8vo, cloth, 6s. With a Frontispiece by Hal Hurst. [*Third Edition. Just out.*

The *DAILY TELEGRAPH* says:—"This thrilling tale. The plot is worked out with remarkable ingenuity. The book abounds in clever and graphic characterisation."

18 *Bouverie Street, Fleet Street, London.*

NEW NOVELS AND STORIES—*Continued.*

NEW NOVEL BY FLORENCE MARRYAT.

The Beautiful Soul. By the Author of "A Fatal Silence," "There is no Death," etc., etc. Crown 8vo, cloth, 6*s.*   [*Fourth Edition.*

The *GUARDIAN* says:—"We read the book with real pleasure and interest. . . . In Felecia Hetherington, Miss Marryat has drawn a really fine character, and has given her what she claims for her in the title, a beautiful soul."
The *WORLD* says:—"An entertaining and animated story. . . . One of the most lovable women to whom novel readers have been introduced."

Une Culotte: An Impossible Story of Modern Oxford. By "Tivoli," Author of "A Defender of the Faith." With Illustrations by A. W. Cooper. Crown 8vo, cloth, 6*s.*   [*Second Edition.*

The *DAILY CHRONICLE* says:—"The book is full of funny things. The story is a screaming farce, and will furnish plenty of amusement."

The Vengeance of Medea. By Edith Gray Wheelwright. Crown 8vo, cloth, 6*s.*

The *WESTERN DAILY MERCURY* says:—"Miss Wheelwright has introduced several delightful characters, and produced a work which will add to her reputation. The dialogue is especially well written."

A Ruined Life. By Emily St Clair. Crown 8vo, cloth, 6*s.*

The *BIRMINGHAM GAZETTE* says:—"A powerful story developed with considerable dramatic skill and remarkable fervour."

The Westovers. By Algernon Ridgeway. Author of "Westover's Ward," "Diana Fontaine," etc. Crown 8vo, cloth, 6*s.*

The *GLASGOW HERALD* says:—"'The Westovers' is a clever book."

The Flaming Sword. Being an Account of the Extraordinary Adventures and Discoveries of Dr Percival in the Wilds of Africa. Written by Himself. Crown 8vo, cloth, 6*s.*

The *SPEAKER* says:—"Mr Rider Haggard himself has not imagined more wonderful things than those which befell Dr Percival and his friends."
The *LITERARY WORLD* says:—"Out-Haggards Haggard."

In Due Season. By Agnes Goldwin. Crown 8vo, cloth, 6*s.*

The *ACADEMY* says:—"Her novel is well written, it flows easily, its situations are natural, its men and women are real."

His Last Amour. By Monopole. Crown 8vo, cloth, 6*s.*

The *GLASGOW HERALD* says:—"The story is unfolded with considerable skill, and the interest of the reader is not allowed to flag."

NEW NOVELS AND STORIES—*Continued.*

An Unknown Power. By CHARLES E. R. BELLAIRS
Crown 8vo, cloth, 6s.

The *BELFAST NORTHERN WHIG* says:—"From start to finish the reader's attention is never allowed to flag. The characters are drawn with considerable fidelity to life. The plot is original, and its developments well worked out."

NEW NOVEL BY GERTRUDE L. WARREN.

The Mystery of Hazelgrove. By GERTRUDE L. WARREN. Crown 8vo, cloth, 6s. [*Just out.*

NEW NOVEL BY ALICE MAUD MEADOWS.

When the Heart is Young. By the Author of "The Romance of a Madhouse," etc. Crown 8vo, cloth. 6s. [*Fourth Edition.*

A NEW AUSTRALIAN NOVEL.

Recognition. A Mystery of the Coming Colony. By SYDNEY H. WRIGHT. Crown 8vo, cloth, 6s. [*Shortly.*

A NEW SPORTING STORY.

With the Bankshire Hounds. By M. F. H. Crown 8vo, cloth, 6s. [*Just out.*

Some Passages in Plantagenet Paul's Life. By HIMSELF. Crown 8vo, cloth, 6s. [*Just out.*

Drifting. By MARSTON MOORE. Crown 8vo, cloth, 6s. [*Just out.*

Coneycreek. By M. LAWSON. Crown 8vo, cloth, 6s. [*Just out.*

IN THREE VOLUMES, Price **31s. 6d.**

BY DORA RUSSELL.

A Hidden Chain. By the Author of "Footprints in the Snow," "The Other Bond," etc., etc. In Three Volumes, crown 8vo, cloth, 31s. 6d. [*Second Edition.*

BY JEAN MIDDLEMASS.

The Mystery of Clement Dunraven. By the Author of "A Girl in a Thousand," etc. In Three Volumes, crown 8vo, cloth, 31s. 6d. [*Second Edition.*

BY PERCY ROSS.

The Eccentrics. By the Author of "A Comedy without Laughter," "A Misguidit Lassie," "A Professor of Alchemy," etc. In Three Volumes, crown 8vo, cloth, 31s. 6d.

NEW NOVELS AND STORIES—*Continued.*

By GILBERTA M. F. LYON.

Absent Yet Present. By the Author of "For Good or Evil." In Three Volumes, crown 8vo, cloth, 31*s.* 6*d.*

By MADELINE CRICHTON.

Like a Sister. In Three Volumes, crown 8vo, cloth, 31*s.* 6*d.*　　　　　　　　　　[*Second Edition.*

IN ONE VOLUME, Price **3s. 6d.**

NEW BOOK BY THE AUTHOR OF "A PLUNGE INTO SPACE."

The Crack of Doom. By ROBERT CROMIE, Author of "For England's Sake," etc. Crown 8vo, cloth, 3*s.* 6*d.*

*** The first Large Edition was exhausted before publication. SECOND EDITION now ready.

Her Loving Slave. By HUME NISBET, author of "The Jolly Roger," "Bail Up," etc., etc. In Handsome Pictorial Binding, with Illustrations by the Author. Crown 8vo, cloth, 3*s.* 6*d.*　　　　[*Third Edition.*

His Egyptian Wife. By HILTON HILL. Crown 8vo, cloth, 3*s.* 6*d.* With Frontispiece.

*** Published simultaneously in London and New York.

A Son of Noah. By MARY ANDERSON, author of "Othello's Occupation." Crown 8vo, cloth, 3*s.* 6*d.*　　　　　　　　　　[*Fifth Edition.*

The Last Cruise of the Teal. By LEIGH RAY. In handsome pictorial binding. Illustrated throughout. Crown 8vo, cloth, 3*s.* 6*d.*　　[*Second Edition.*
The *NATIONAL OBSERVER* says :—"It is long since we have lighted on so good a story of adventure."

His Troublesome Sister. By EVA TRAVERS EVERED POOLE, Author of many Popular Stories. Crown 8vo, cloth, 3*s.* 6*d.*
The *BIRMINGHAM POST* says:—"An interesting and well-constructed story. The characters are strongly drawn, the plot is well devised, and those who commence the book will be sure to finish it."

The Bow and the Sword. A Romance. By E. C. ADAMS, M.A. With 16 full-page drawings by MATTHEW STRETCH. Crown 8vo, pictorial cloth, 3*s.* 6*d.*
The *MORNING POST* says:—"The author reconstructs cleverly the life of one of the most cultivated nations of antiquity, and describes both wars and pageants with picturesque vigour. The illustrations are well executed."

---

18 Bouverie Street, Fleet Street, London.

NEW NOVELS AND STORIES—*Continued.*

The Maid of Havodwen. By JOHN FERRARS.

Author of "Claud Brennan." Crown 8vo, cloth, 3*s.* 6*d.*

The *DUNDEE ADVERTISER* says :—"A charming story of Welsh life and character. . . . Deeply interesting. . . . Of unusual attractiveness."

Paths that Cross. By MARK TREHERN. Crown 8vo, cloth, 3*s.* 6*d.*

The *DAILY TELEGRAPH* says:—"Cleverly sketched characters. The book is enlivened throughout with innumerable light touches of quaint and spontaneous humour."

A Tale of Two Curates. By Rev. JAMES COPNER, M.A. Crown 8vo, cloth, 3*s.* 6*d.*

The *DUNDEE ADVERTISER* says:—"Simply but graphically narrated."

The Wrong of Fate. By LILLIAS LOBENHOFFER, Author of "Bairnie," etc. Crown 8vo, cloth, 3*s.* 6*d.*

The *LONDON STAR* says:—"A well-written and clever novel, excellent studies of Scotch character."
The *SCOTSMAN* says:—"Shows considerable power."

Studies in Miniature. By A TITULAR VICAR. Crown 8vo, cloth, 3*s.* 6*d.*

The *MANCHESTER COURIER* says :—"Brightly and cleverly written."
The *BELFAST NEWS LETTER* says :—"Very readable, characters admirably drawn."

Spunyarn. By N. J. PRESTON. Crown 8vo, pictorial cloth, 3*s.* 6*d.* [*Just out.*

IN ONE VOLUME, Price 2s. 6d.

Lost! £100 Reward. By MIRIAM YOUNG, Author of "The Girl Musician." Crown 8vo, cloth, 2*s.* 6*d.*

The *WEEKLY SUN* says:—"The interest is well sustained throughout, and the incidents are most graphically described."

Clenched Antagonisms. By LEWIS IRAM. Crown 8vo, cloth, 2*s.* 6*d.*

The *SATURDAY REVIEW* says :—"'Clenched Antagonisms' is a powerful and ghastly narrative of the triumph of force over virtue. The book gives a striking illustration of the barbarous incongruities that still exist in the midst of an advanced civilisation."

For Marjory's Sake : A Story of South Australian Country Life. By Mrs JOHN WATERHOUSE. In handsome cloth binding, with Illustrations. Crown 8vo, cloth, 2*s.* 6*d.*

The *LITERARY WORLD* says:—"A delightful little volume, fresh and dainty, and with the pure, free air of Australian country parts blowing through it . . . gracefully told . . . the writing is graceful and easy."

IN ONE VOLUME, PAPER COVER, Price **1s.**

A Stock Exchange Romance. By BRACEBRIDGE HEMYNG, Author of "The Stockbroker's Wife," "Called to the Bar," etc., etc. Edited by GEORGE GREGORY. Crown 8vo, picture cover, 1s. (TENTH THOUSAND.)

Our Discordant Life. By ADAM D'HÉRISTAL. Crown 8vo, picture cover, 1s.

A Police Sergeant's Secret. By KILSYTH STELLIER, Author of "Taken by Force." Crown 8vo, picture cover, 1s. (FIFTH THOUSAND.)

Irish Stew. By JAMES J. MORAN, Author of "A Deformed Idol," "The Dunferry Risin'," "Runs in the Blood," etc. Crown 8vo, lithographed cover, price 1s.
The *WEEKLY SUN* says:—"Mr MORAN is the 'Barrie' of Ireland. . . . In a remote district in the west of Ireland he has created an Irish Thrums."

La Lecsinska. A Powerful and Clever Novel. By HARRIET BUCKLEY. Crown 8vo, paper cover, 1s.
[*Just out.*

That Other Fellow. An Original and Absorbing Novel. By Mrs LOUISA LE BAILLY. Crown 8vo, paper cover, 1s.
[*Just out.*

DIGBY'S POPULAR NOVEL SERIES.

In Handsome Cloth Binding, Gold Lettered, Cr. 8vo, 320 pp. Price **2s. 6d.** *each, or in Picture Boards, Price* **2s.** *each.*

BY JEAN MIDDLEMASS.

THE MYSTERY OF CLEMENT DUNRAVEN. By the Author of "A Girl in a Thousand," etc. (SECOND EDITION.)

BY DORA RUSSELL.

A HIDDEN CHAIN. By the Author of "Footprints in the Snow," etc. (SECOND EDITION.)

BY DR. A. KENEALY.

Dr JANET OF HARLEY STREET. By the Author of "Molly and her Man-o'-War," etc. (SEVENTH EDITION.) With Portrait.

BY HUME NISBET.

THE JOLLY ROGER. By the Author of "Bail Up," etc. With Illustrations by the Author. (FIFTH EDITION.)

NOTE.—Other Works in the same Series in due course.

MISCELLANEOUS.

A History of the Great Western Railway from Its Inception to the Present Time.

By G. A. SEKON. Revised by F. G. SAUNDERS, Chairman of the Great Western Railway. Demy 8vo, 390 pages, cloth, 7s. 6d. With numerous Illustrations.

** Illustrated Prospectus, post free. [*Second Edition.*

The *TIMES*, April 12th, 1895.—" Mr Sekon's volume is full of interest, and constitutes an important chapter in the history of railway development in England."

The *STANDARD* (Leader), April 4th, 1895.—" An excellent addition to the literature of our iron roads."

The *DAILY TELEGRAPH*, April 13th, 1895.—"Mr G. A. Sekon has performed a service to the public. His book is full of interest, and is evidently the result of a great deal of painstaking inquiry. . . . His book is made all the more valuable by several pictures of engines, collisions, the Saltash Bridge, the Old Bath Station and the Box Tunnel; and it will be welcomed by all interested in the history and extraordinary expansion of our iron roadways."

Three Empresses.

Josephine, Marie-Louise, Eugénie. By CAROLINE GEAREY, Author of "In Other Lands," etc. With portraits. Cr. 8vo, cloth, 6s. (SECOND EDIT.)

The *PALL MALL GAZETTE* says:—" This charming book. . . . Gracefully and graphically written, the story of each Empress is clearly and fully told. . . This delightful book."

Winter and Summer Excursions in Canada.

By C. L. JOHNSTONE, Author of " Historical Families of Dumfriesshire," etc. With Illustrations. Crown 8vo, cloth, 6s.

The *DAILY NEWS* says:—" Not for a long while have we read a book of its class which deserves so much confidence. Intending settlers would do well to study Mr Johnstone's book."

The Author's Manual.

By PERCY RUSSELL. With Prefatory Remarks by Mr GLADSTONE. Crown 8vo, cloth, 3s. 6d. net. (EIGHTH AND CHEAPER EDITION.) With portrait.

The *WESTMINSTER REVIEW* says:—". . Mr Russell's book is a very complete manual and guide for journalist and author. It is not a merely practical work—It is literary and appreciative of literature in its best sense; . . . we have little else but praise for the volume."

A Guide to British and American Novels.

From the Earliest Period to the end of 1894. By PERCY RUSSELL, Author of "The Author's Manual," etc. Crown 8vo, cloth. Price 3s. 6d. net. (SECOND EDITION CAREFULLY REVISED.)

The *SPECTATOR* says:—" Mr Russell's familiarity with every form of novel is amazing, and his summaries of plots and comments thereon are as brief and lucid as they are various."

MISCELLANEOUS—*Continued.*

Sixty Years' Experience as an Irish Landlord.

Memoirs of JOHN HAMILTON, D.L. of St Ernan's, Donegal. Edited, with Introduction, by the Rev. H C. WHITE, late Chaplain, Paris. Crown 8vo, cloth, 6s. With Portrait.

The *TIMES* says:—"Much valuable light on the real history of Ireland, and of the Irish agrarian question in the present century is thrown by a very interesting volume entitled 'Sixty Years' Experience as an Irish Landlord.' . . . This very instructive volume."

Nigh on Sixty Years at Sea. By ROBERT WOOL-

WARD ("Old Woolward"). Crown 8vo, cloth, 6s. With Portrait. (SECOND EDITION.)

The *TIMES* says:—"Very entertaining reading. Captain Woolward writes sensibly and straightforwardly, and tells his story with the frankness of an old salt. He has a keen sense of humour, and his stories are endless and very entertaining."

Whose Fault? The Story of a Trial at *Nisi Prius.*

By ELLIS J. DAVIS, Barrister-at-Law. In handsome pictorial binding. Crown 8vo, cloth, 3s. 6d.

The *TIMES* says:—"An ingenious attempt to convey to the lay mind an accurate and complete idea of the origin and progress and all the essential circumstances of an ordinary action at law. The idea is certainly a good one, and is executed in very entertaining fashion. . . . Mr Davis's instructive little book."

Borodin and Liszt. I.—Life and Works of a Russian

Composer. II.—Liszt, as sketched in the Letters of Borodin. By ALFRED HABETS. Translated with a Preface by ROSA NEWMARCH. With Portraits and Fac-similes. [*Just out.*

Fragments from Victor Hugo's Legends and Lyrics. By CECILIA ELIZABETH MEETKERKE.

Crown 8vo, cloth, 7s. 6d.

The *WORLD* says:—"The most admirable rendering of French poetry into English that has come to our knowledge since Father Prout's translation of 'La Chant du Cosaque.'"

BY THE AUTHOR OF "SONG FAVOURS."

Minutiæ. By CHARLES WILLIAM DALMON. Royal

16mo, cloth elegant, price 2s. 6d.

The *ACADEMY* says:—"His song has a rare and sweet note. The little book has colour and fragrance, and is none the less welcome because the fragrance is delicate, evanescent; the colours of white and silver grey and lavender, rather than brilliant and exuberant. . . . Mr Dalmon's genuine artistry. In his sonnets he shows a deft touch, particularly in the fine one, 'Ecce Ancilla Domini.' Yet, after all, it is in the lyrics that he is most individual. . . . Let him take heart, for surely the song that he has to sing is worth singing."

⁎⁎ *A complete Catalogue of Novels, Travels, Biographies, Poems, etc., with a critical or descriptive notice of each, free by post on application.*

London: **DIGBY, LONG & CO.**, Publishers,
18 *Bouverie Street, Fleet Street, E.C.*

www.ingramcontent.com/pod-product-compliance
Lightning Source LLC
Chambersburg PA
CBHW030132030726

47498CB00007B/2670